P9-DER-216

DISCARDED AND
WITHDRAWN FROM
WARWICK PUBLIC
LIBRARY

ALSO BY BRENDAN HALPIN

Forever Changes
How Ya Like Me Now

SHUTOUT

SHUTOUT

BRENDAN HALPIN

FARRAR STRAUS GIROUX

NEW YORK

Copyright © 2010 by Brendan Halpin
All rights reserved
Distributed in Canada by D&M Publishers, Inc.
Printed in October 2010 in the United States of America
by RR Donnelley & Sons Company, Harrisonburg, Virginia
Designed by Robbin Gourley
First edition, 2010
3   5   7   9   10   8   6   4   2

www.fsgkidsbooks.com

Library of Congress Cataloging-in-Publication Data
Halpin, Brendan, 1968–
    Shutout / Brendan Halpin.— 1st ed.
        p.   cm.
    Summary: Fourteen-year-old Amanda and her best friend Lena start
high school looking forward to playing on the varsity soccer team, but
when Lena makes varsity and Amanda only makes junior varsity, their
long friendship rapidly changes.
    ISBN: 978-0-374-36899-9
    [1. Soccer—Fiction.   2. Friendship—Fiction.   3. Interpersonal
relations—Fiction.   4. Family life—Massachusetts—Fiction.   5. High
schools—Fiction.   6. Schools—Fiction.]   I. Title.

PZ7.H16674Sh 2010
[Fic]—dc22

                                                    2009032972

To Casey, Rowen, and Kylie

Warm-up

I started playing soccer and being friends with Lena in the third grade; six years later, they both turned on me.

Well, my body turned on me first. I'm not talking about developing embarrassing boobs and monthly bleeding and hair in gross places. That stuff happens to everybody. What happened to me is Sever's disease.

I love saying that because it sounds really dramatic and life-threatening, like I have a disease that's going to cause part of me to get cut off. If you tell a group of people that you have Sever's disease, they will make these sad noises at you and tell you how brave you are and stuff like that, which is pretty funny because they actually have no idea what the hell it is.

What it actually is is heel pain. See why I like saying Sever's disease instead? Heel pain sounds so wimpy, no matter how you dress it up. I can tell you that after I play soccer, it feels like there's somebody constantly shoving an eight-inch kitchen knife into the back of my heel, and still it doesn't sound as dramatic as Sever's disease.

Sever's disease is a condition where your bones grow really fast, and your muscles and tendons can't keep up. So these short muscles and tendons in your legs get stretched out until they're really tight, and they pull on the back of your heel until it feels like somebody's just whacked you on the bottom of your foot with a hammer.

I know that compared to cystic fibrosis or cancer or any of the other million horrible diseases I could have, Sever's disease is a pretty easy ride. The best part is that it's completely curable. The worst part is that the only cure is reaching your full height. I'm fourteen years old and five feet ten inches tall, which is already totally freakish for a girl, so I'm going to be pretty pissed if I don't stop growing soon.

My mom understands this pretty well—she gets how hard it is to fit in, how they don't make clothes for girls my size, especially shoes (you try finding something that isn't hideous in a size *eleven*), and she's always really good about listening to all my complaints and sympathizing. I guess she was fat in high school, which you'd never know to look at her now, but anyway, she gets how tough it is to be a teenage girl.

Of course, she's also not my mom. Well, she kind of is. It's complicated. I think of her as my mom, and she's the only mom I can ever remember having, but she didn't give birth to me. My biological mom died when I was two. She was five feet eleven inches tall, which is pretty funny because my dad is only five six. So you can imagine what they looked like together. She wore flats to their wedding and still totally towered over him.

So the fact that my mom was a freakish giantess (I'm sorry, Mom I Don't Remember, but it's just the truth. And yeah, it takes one to know one) means that Dad sees my own freakish gigantism as some kind of great gift because it makes me Mom's—my late mom, I mean the dead one—walking tombstone or something. Every once in a while I catch him looking up at me all misty-eyed, and one time I made the mistake of going, "What?" and Dad was like, "It's nothing. It's just that you looked so much like your mom there for a second." Stupid me for asking. Now I always know what he's thinking when he looks at me that way, and it's annoying.

So Dad gets all mad when I complain about my height, but then Mom—the alive one—tells him he has no idea how mean girls can be, and Dad says he damn sure does. That's why he stayed in basements playing Dungeons and Dragons with his geeky friends until he was sixteen, which is a pretty funny picture. I mean, I think about my parents in high school—Dad pale, skinny, and short, sitting in some dork's basement, and Mom all fat and standing on the wall at every dance hoping to get a pity dance out of somebody, and it kind of gives me hope. I mean, they survived high school and seem to be pretty happy grownups, so I guess I probably will too.

It's not always easy to take that point of view, though. In fact, it's almost always impossible to take that point of view. Especially after they made the cut.

Preseason

1

Lena slept over. Except for the times when we were on our separate little family vacations, we spent most of the summer together, and we probably slept at each other's houses two or three times a week. Lena likes to come to my house because her parents are nuts, I mean even in comparison to most parents. Also she has a crush on my brother. The one who's fifteen. I mean my stepbrother, except we never use the "step" part unless we're in a really big fight. The kid sees his dad like three weeks a year. We've lived together for forty-nine weeks a year since I was four, so it seems dumb to say he's anything but my brother. I have another brother, Dominic, who's eight, but he's actually my half brother, and Conrad's half brother too. Neither of us ever uses the "half" with Dominic no matter how annoying he is, which is very.

But I was talking about Conrad, my brother who has, I know from when he recently mooned me, developed butt hair, which is just about the grossest thing I can imagine. I'm pretty sure I'm into guys, sexual orientation–wise, but the sight of Conrad's hairy butt really made me question for a while whether that was a good idea. I mean, if I remain heterosexual, I will presumably be called on at some point to be naked with a guy, and he might have a hairy butt. I really can't imagine being so into anyone that I could overlook that.

I guess it's possible that Conrad is just a freak of nature and the only guy on earth who has butt hair. Well, he's certainly a freak of nature, but I don't know if that means he's the only guy with butt hair or not. Okay, this is really grossing me out. Let me talk about something else.

Like how Lena was over the night before the cut. We had both been playing our hearts out at soccer practice all week. Some people complained about working that hard in the hot August sun, but we were into that part of summer where the vacations are over and there's really nothing going on except worrying about school starting, so I was happy to have something to do.

And I loved soccer. It was fun, and I was good at it. Well, sort of. I mean, before the whole Sever's disease thing hit, Lena and I were a great offensive team. We'd charge up the field together, her in the center, me on the wing, passing all the way until one of us drew the defenders. Then it was cross to the other one, goal. It never even mattered to either of us which of us actually put the ball in the goal—they were all *our* goals. I remember Lena coming over after a game one day and when Dad, who'd been at Conrad's game, asked how we did, we both said, "We scored three goals!" in unison.

It seems kind of corny now, not to mention unbelievable

that we didn't care which of us had two goals and which had one, but that's really how it was.

But then Sever's disease came to visit right about the time they moved us to playing on a bigger field, and suddenly I went from charging up the wing and crossing to my best friend to hobbling toward the goal, watching defenders pick off a pass I couldn't catch up to.

Still, I was lucky, because back then I had Lori as a coach. I was moping after one game because we would have had a chance to tie if I had been able to catch up to Lena's pass, but I couldn't, so we lost. Lori took me aside and said, "I want to ask you something."

"Yeah?"

"What do you think about playing goal?"

"Honestly? I kind of think it sucks. If I wanted to stand around waiting for something to happen, I would have signed up for softball."

"Well, listen," she said, "you have a gift for this game. And I know right now you can't run the way you'd like to, but I know you've scored enough goals that you can read people, when they're going to pass and when they're going to shoot and even where the ball is going."

"Um. Thanks. I mean, yeah, I guess I get that stuff."

"If you want to, I'll be happy to work with you on this. I know you can be as strong a goalkeeper as you were a forward."

Well, that was a pretty good pep talk, and so I did work with Lori on goalkeeping, and I got Lena to shoot on me all the time. Pretty soon we were the Twin Towers—Lena in the front and me in the back, and our team was unstoppable. Well, we would have been the Twin Towers, but Lena's only five feet four inches tall. So, okay, I was a tower and she was a Ferrari.

I guess this is going to sound conceited, but we were good enough that I didn't think it was crazy to hope we'd make varsity as ninth graders.

All the girls hoping to make the high school teams had been practicing together for the last two weeks, and whenever Lena and I got to play in a scrimmage, we were just as good as we'd always been. And Lena was unstoppable when we ran—I don't know how she goes so fast on her short legs, but she's easily the fastest girl on the team, including some of the senior girls who have these incredible muscly tree trunk thighs.

I, of course, can barely run at all before I start limping. But I did the right thing and talked to one of the coaches, Ms. Beasley, who is the younger and nicer of the two, about Sever's disease and how I'm probably almost done growing, so it shouldn't be a factor for long. I do have a hard time running, I said, but just watch me in the goal.

She made sure I got in the goal during scrimmages, and I saw her talking to scary, crusty Ms. Keezer whenever I made a save. Maybe she was just trying to tell Ms. Keezer about sunblock and moisturizers and how you could be a female sports coach without looking like a dried-up apple doll. But I hope she was talking about my awesome saves.

Anyway, it was the last day before they made the cut, and Lena was sleeping over. She was mad cheesy all night, trying to involve Conrad in conversations and stuff, and he is either clueless about Lena liking him, which is hard to imagine since she's so obvious about it, or else he doesn't like her, which is also hard to imagine since she's pretty and smart and grew a cup size in like a weekend this summer.

Or maybe he likes her and just doesn't know what to do about it, which is totally fine with me, because the two of them together would make my life awkward, not to mention gross.

Lena and I were in sleeping bags in a tent in the basement (yes, we're corny, and yes, there are perfectly good beds upstairs, but we have more privacy to talk in the basement and besides we like to have these little imaginary campouts like we're six years old). We were talking about the cut.

"I think we're both gonna make it," Lena said.

"I don't know," I answered. "Remember that big speech Ms. Beasley gave about how the younger players almost never make varsity and we have to pay dues and blah blah?"

"Yeah, but, I mean, not to be conceited, but we are pretty good. I feel like we're definitely in the top half of the girls there," Lena said.

"Yeah." I hoped that was true, but it was hard to believe with all these senior girls running around being awesome.

"Well," I said, "I think we'll probably only make JV, but that'll be cool because we'll get to play a lot, and we'll be together."

"Yeah," Lena said. "But it would be even cooler if we were together on varsity."

"Yeah," I agreed, "it would." We lay there for a while not talking, and even though I kept telling myself that ninth graders almost never make varsity, I could see the whole thing clearly—Lena up front, me in the goal, all the way to the state championship. The team had missed going to states last year, but this year they'd have the crucial puzzle pieces in place: us. We'd be just what they needed to push the team to the next level.

"What are you thinking about?" Lena asked.

"I was just imagining winning the state championship."

"I would totally take off my shirt like Brandi Chastain," Lena said.

I laughed. "I think you might get suspended if you did that."

"Well, we could both do it," she answered. "Then it would be like this great team moment of triumph, and even if we got suspended we could hang out and watch *Bend It Like Beckham* all day."

"Yeah, you know, I think I'd rather not turn this great moment of triumph into a great moment of humiliation when I strip off my shirt and everybody points and laughs and the league makes me pee in a cup to prove I'm female." Yeah, boobs are embarrassing, but I think actual boobs would be somewhat less embarrassing than these little pointy nubs I've got.

Lena laughed. "You so need a confidence boost, girl. I swear I have no idea how you look in the mirror and see what you see."

"A gigantic freak?"

"Yeah, that's what *you* see. *I* see this pretty girl with a supermodel body and a brain in her head that guys are going to be totally falling for next week."

"You sound like my dad," I said.

"I didn't say anything about you looking like somebody who's dead," Lena answered, and that was one of those things your best friend can say and it's funny and if anybody else said it you'd want to punch them.

"I guess you're right. Well, thanks. That's a nice fantasy. Almost as good as us making varsity and winning states."

"It's gonna happen," Lena said. "Just wait till tomorrow."

I drifted off to sleep imagining saving the tying goal in the state championship while my own personal cheering section of really tall guys—maybe the basketball team?—watched from the stands and held up homemade signs with my name on them.

2

We got up early, and Lena made goo-goo eyes at Conrad across the breakfast table while he read the sports section. It made me slightly nauseous, and I might not have eaten, but I knew we'd be running all day and I'd need my strength.

"So, did the Sox win?" Lena asked.

"Four–three over the Jays," Conrad replied as he took another bite of a poppy seed bagel. He had these little smears of cream cheese with dots of poppy seeds on his cheeks. He looked completely ridiculous. I thought about saying something to him, but I was afraid he might give one of his typical responses, like "And you've got something really ugly on top of your neck—oh, snap, it's your face!" Moron. How could Lena possibly like him? She was frantically trying to find something, anything else, to say after Mr. Scintillating Conversation had relayed the score of last night's game, but Mom came in and shut her down, or possibly saved her from saying some awkward, embarrassing thing that she'd kick herself for later.

"You girls all ready for your big day?" Mom asked, making herself a cup of herbal tea. I guess she had a big meeting or something, because she was wearing a suit. I looked at her and tried not to think about how unfair it was that I would never inherit those curves.

"Sure," I said. "You look great, by the way."

"You think? I was feeling like this skirt made me look a little hippy."

"At least you have hips," I answered.

Mom smiled. "Okay, Manda, you and I can play dueling bad body image later, maybe when Conrad's not around."

"Like he notices." I pointed to Conrad, who was still completely lost in the sports section.

"Point taken, but it's still bad form. Lena, how are you feeling about today?"

"Okay. Nervous," she said.

"Well, you girls are great, but just remember how high school sports work. Seniors are going to get those varsity spots, and it's the right thing for the coaches to do. You'll want it that way when you're a senior."

I rolled my eyes. "Yeah, we heard that the first five times you said it, Mom."

Mom smiled. "Okay, okay. It's going to be hot today— make sure you take two water bottles each."

Lena and I held up our huge bottles, already filled with ice water. "Excellent, girls. You have to stay hydrated. What about you, Conrad?" Mom asked.

Silence, and we all stared at Conrad, who stared at the paper.

"Conrad?" Mom waited for a minute, and when he showed no signs of having heard her, she raised her voice. "Conrad!"

He looked up. "You don't have to yell, Mom, God, I'm right here!"

"Obviously she did have to yell because you totally didn't answer her the first three times she asked you," I said.

Mom turned to me. "Amanda, don't parent. That's my job. Conrad, I just wanted to know if you have enough water for practice today."

"Yeah, my water bottle's in my room somewhere."

Mom took a deep breath. "We have a bin for all your soccer stuff. If you just used it, then you'd always know where your water bottle was."

"Got it, Mom, thanks," Conrad said as he disappeared into the paper again. Mom looked like she wanted to yell at him, but instead she topped up her travel mug and turned to go.

"Okay, I'm gonna be late," she said. "I love you all, have a great day, and remember that whatever happens, none of this is a referendum on your worth as people."

Five minutes later, Lena and I were on our way to the high school fields. My stomach felt tight and sour. I hoped I wouldn't puke. I was so nervous, which was stupid. I mean, most ninth graders get put on JV, no questions asked. I guess I thought if I made varsity, then when school started next week I would already be somebody.

Well, I would be somebody no matter what. I just thought it might be nice to be somebody besides the hugely tall ninth grade girl getting lost in the halls and feeling totally out of place. If I were on varsity, I'd be in with a lot of older girls, so

I'd have a friendly face to ask if I had any questions, and when people talked about me, they would say how I must be a hell of a soccer player to make varsity as a ninth grader. Going into this new school with all these new people, I wanted to be somebody besides the Tallest Girl in the Class.

That's what I was thinking about on the way to practice. Lena, of course, was thinking about Conrad, who rode past us on his bike with a friendly "Later, losers." "I don't know, I think maybe he might like me."

"Why?"

"Well, did you see how long it took him to answer your mom? He was completely tuned out, but he answered me right away. Right? So, like, my voice is important to him or something. Right?"

"I think he was ignoring Mom just to be a dick, but okay," I said.

"Maybe you could ask him," she kind of half whispered.

"You want me to tell him you like him?"

"Oh my God no. That would be so embarrassing. I don't know, I thought there might be a way . . ."

"You might not have noticed this, but we don't really talk about who we like, or much of anything else with each other," I said.

"Okay. Well, let me know if he does say anything."

"Will do."

We didn't say much else on the way to practice—I guess we were both obsessing.

We got to practice right on time, and everybody else was already there. The boys' soccer team was doing their usual thing where they stand around pretending to stretch while looking at the girls. But we were not doing what we usually do, which is pass and shoot and pretend not to notice the boys, especially that Duncan kid who's in the tenth grade and is almost too gorgeous to be real. I swear to God the guy must be an android or, like, an alien from Planet Hot or something.

Instead of pretending to ignore the boys, all the girls actually were ignoring the boys, sitting on the ground staring at crusty Ms. Keezer, who was standing there looking stern and holding a clipboard. She glared at me and Lena as we sat down. I looked at Ms. Beasley, and she gave me a friendly smile.

Ms. Keezer looked at her watch. "It's nine o'clock," she yelled in her scratchy, raspy voice, "and we have a lot of work to do today, so we're going to get this out of the way early. Ms. Beasley and I have made the decision about which girls are going to which squad. Listen carefully for your name as Ms. Beasley reads the JV list. Those of you on JV will be coached by Ms. Beasley, and you'll be practicing with her today. I'll be coaching varsity. Now, the school committee in their infinite wisdom forbids us from holding practice over Labor Day weekend, and our first games of the season are next Wednesday, which means we have only two practices between now and then. We need all of our practice time to try to get ready to compete by next week, so if you want to have a long, involved conversation about how our placement isn't fair and we should reconsider, please put your complaint in writing, and I'll make sure it gets filed appropriately." She shook a big plastic garbage can as she said this, and all the senior girls who knew they were making varsity anyway laughed, and the rest of us felt sick. Or maybe that was just me.

Ms. Beasley started reading names. It was alphabetical order, so it didn't take her long to get to Amanda Conant. (Yeah, I've heard the "Conant the Barbarian" joke a few times. Funny stuff.) Lena reached over and squeezed my hand as we waited for her name. Well, making varsity as a ninth grader was a stupid dream anyway, and at least we'd have the nice young coach instead of the scary old one.

Ms. Beasley read a bunch of other names, finishing up with Shakina Williams. Then she said, "Okay, if you heard your name, come with me. If you didn't, you'll stay here with Ms. Keezer, and congratulations." She took her clipboard and a bunch of girls got up immediately to follow her, and I sat there still squeezing the hand of Lena Zaleski, whose name hadn't been called.

"Maybe my name was on the second page or something," Lena said. "This has to be a mistake. Let's go ask her." We dropped hands and stood up, and Ms. Keezer barked, "Zaleski! Sit!" and Lena—fast, beautiful, and a normal female height—sat back down with this "I'm sorry" look on her face while I walked toward Ms. Beasley and the Loser Squad and tried really hard not to cry.

3

My dad is a hopeless cornball, which I guess is why I tend to talk more to my mom about personal stuff. But sometimes I wonder if my dad is some sort of evil genius, because a lot of times he says some dumb thing that's so corny it makes me want to curl up under the table and disappear, but then later on I'll hear him saying it in my brain and it kind of makes sense to me.

One of his favorite things is to talk about how tough I am because my mom died. I mean, like I even remember that. I was two. But anyway, whenever something feels hard for me and I'm doing a bad job of hiding it, he'll say something like this, usually with his voice breaking: "Amanda, you are the strongest person I know. You've been through stuff most kids can only imagine, and you'll get through this too. Compared to what's already happened in your life, this is a walk in the park, and I know you can do it. You're tough as an old boot."

Like any fourteen-year-old girl wants to be compared to a

battered piece of leather. Though maybe that comparison gets more appropriate as you get older, because Ms. Keezer actually does look kind of like an old boot.

Anyway, as I was standing in the goal trying not to hear the happy practice going on at the other end of the field, as I was trying really hard to just focus on the ball and not think about how humiliated and sad and jealous I felt, how Lena was already prettier and more girlish than me, and now she was a better soccer player too, I heard my dad's voice in my mind.

"You are the strongest person I know," he said, and I punched away a ball like it was Ms. Keezer's gross dried-up head.

"You're tough as an old boot," he said as I leaped across the goal and grabbed a ball I guessed wrong on and got to anyway.

I managed to get through the rest of practice this way, and I managed not to cry, even at the end when, as we were all packing up and Ms. Beasley was handing out the no-substance-abuse pledge forms for us to sign, she came up to me and whispered, "I'm really lucky to have the best goalkeeper on my team."

That was nice, but obviously not true, because the best goalkeeper gets to be on varsity, along with the best forward. Ms. Keezer was keeping her team, the good, non-loser team, late, and the best goalkeeper was practicing over there while I walked home. And, oh yeah, all the boys were lingering over by the varsity girls, totally ignoring those of us who didn't make the cut.

I saw Mrs. Zaleski in the parking lot. I practically lived at

Lena's house when she wasn't practically living at mine, and even though Mrs. Zaleski is not as warm as my mom and never randomly tells us she loves us and she's proud of us when we're over there, she's still probably the adult outside of my own family that I know the best. So when she smiled and waved at me, I knew I should go over there and say hi to her, especially since they were leaving for the weekend right after practice, but I couldn't do it. Because what could she possibly say to make it better? And I could just about hold it together if I didn't talk about it, but if I did have to say something, I knew I would start crying.

So I just waved and kept walking.

4

It's only a couple of blocks from the field to our house, but of course something happened on the way home too, because it was that kind of day. I was walking with my ball under my arm, and some loser on a bike came by and punched it. The ball rolled into the street right when somebody was driving by in their big stupid SUV they probably had to expand their garage for, and they squashed the ball flat.

We have lots of balls at home, so it's not like it was some irreplaceable family heirloom or something, but I just didn't have it in me to be tough about anything anymore, so I sat down on the sidewalk and started to cry.

At this point the idiot loser on the bike who had played the hilarious prank on me came wheeling back, I guess to rub my nose in how hilarious his prank was.

Oh, did I mention that the idiot loser was my *step*brother, Conrad?

So there I was crying on the sidewalk, and Conrad came over on his bike. I ignored him.

"Hey," he said.

I didn't raise my head or any part of my body other than my middle finger.

"It's just a ball, Amanda, God," he said. I knew this was the part where I yelled at him and we had a big fight, but I didn't have the energy to do anything but cry. I guess this must have caught him off-guard because he didn't say anything for a while.

Then, finally, he said, "I'm sorry. I wasn't trying to wreck it or anything."

Now I did look up at him, because his stupidity was offensive to me. "Well, what did you think was going to happen? I mean, did you think about the fact that we're right next to a street with cars on it, and that rolling balls can actually get squished by two-ton machines?"

He didn't say anything for a second. Then he practically whispered, "Um. I didn't really think about that, no. I just thought it would be funny."

"Well, it's hilarious. Almost as funny as me getting cut from varsity."

"Oh. I'm sorry about that. But you know they really don't ever put ninth graders on varsity. I mean, for somebody to be on varsity in the ninth grade, they'd have to be like Mia Hamm or somebody, but for normal humans—"

"Lena made it."

His reaction to this news was enough to make me take the "step" away, at least for a minute.

"What?" he yelled. "That is total bullshit! I can't believe that! She's good, but she's not better than you. That is so stupid! God, Geezer must have had her brains fried by the sun."

This was enough to get a laugh out of me. "Geezer?"

Conrad looked at me like I was from outer space. "Oh my God, you've never heard that? Everybody calls her that."

"Not at soccer practice they don't."

"Yeah, well, in the real world, they do. She's all old and crinkly, and her name rhymes . . . it's a pretty obvious joke." He held out his hand to me and helped me up. Then he got off his bike and walked with me the rest of the way home, fuming about Geezer's idiocy the whole way.

"You know what it is, right? It's freakin' Stephanie LoPresto. She's a senior, so they have to put her on varsity, but she's a sieve in the goal. They would have totally made states with you in the goal. They'll be lucky to win the conference with her back there. They might as well just pull the goalie altogether and put another forward in."

Of course I would never tell him this, but it was really nice to have Conrad on my side for a change. It seemed like we'd been fighting more or less nonstop since I was ten, and it felt good to get a break from that on a day when I totally couldn't deal with it. It should have been comforting to know I hadn't made the team because of some senior girl, but it wasn't. Because if I wasn't afflicted with Sever's disease, then I would be able to run and I could play another position and maybe be a backup goalie. It was so unfair.

We got home and Conrad went over to the bulkhead to park his bike in the basement and I headed in the front door.

I wanted to run up to my room and cry, but Dad and Dominic were home playing Mario Party. I looked in the living room and rolled my eyes. Because, okay, you expect to see your annoying eight-year-old brother there in front of the TV frantically pounding on the controller, but when your forty-three-year-old father is doing the same thing, it's just embarrassing.

It's also embarrassing when your dad pumps his fist at your eight-year-old brother and goes, in this weird accent, "Waluigi the winner!"

He looked up at me after video game trash-talking his son and didn't look the least bit ashamed. "Hey, sweetie!" he said. "How was practice?"

I was going to give him the standard "Fine," and head upstairs for a good sulk (which, for once, was not going to include calling Lena, because she couldn't understand what I was feeling), but unfortunately, Conrad came up from the basement at that point. He was holding a box of latex gloves in his hand, and he kind of shook them at Dad and said, "She didn't make varsity. And Lena did! Can you believe this crap?"

Dad looked over at Conrad and asked, "Why are you holding a box of gloves?"

Conrad looked at his hand like he'd forgotten they were even there. "Oh. I don't know. I guess I must have picked them up in the basement."

"Cool!" Dominic shouted. "Let's fill 'em up with milk and make udders to drink out of."

"Awesome!" Conrad said, and he and Dominic went running to the kitchen.

All Dad said to them was "Make sure they're the powder-free kind, guys." I really wished Mom was home at that point. When it's just me in the house with three boys, I start wondering if it's them or me who's completely insane, and when Mom's here, I can be confident in the knowledge that it's them.

Dad looked at me with his concerned face. "I'm sorry, sweetie," he said. "I know how much that hurts."

"Dad, you never played soccer in your life."

"Yeah, but I had . . . did I ever tell you the story of *Romeo and Juliet* senior year?"

"You mean about how the screen fell down and the whole school accidentally saw that girl's butt you had a crush on?"

"It was her whole self I had a crush on, not just her butt, but no, that's not the story."

Every single thing that ever happens, Dad has a story. I knew I was going to have to hear it eventually, so I figured I might as well get it over with. "Okay, what was it?"

"Well, you know Uncle Jake was in that play too?"

"Yeah?" Jake's not really Dad's brother, but he's always been Uncle Jake to me.

"He was my best friend then as he is now, and we were both seniors, so, you know, we had a reasonable expectation that we'd get big parts. And we did. Jake was Romeo and I was Friar Lawrence." He had this look on his face like he'd said something important.

"So?"

"So? So my best friend gets to play the tragic romantic hero, and I get to play the old buffoon! How do you think that feels? He got more dates than me anyway, and here's our director, a respected adult—well, after hearing about all the—"

I rolled my eyes. "Dad? The point?"

"Right. So here's this respected adult who hands down this decision that says, essentially, you, Jake, are an attractive young man, and you, Dan, are so far from attractive that you can play an old celibate buffoon. I know it probably sounds stupid, but it hurt. A lot. There are other parts in that play for young men—Mercutio is a great part and he also gets to die tragically, Tybalt is this hotheaded brawler, and he gets to die too, but no, I had to be the cowardly old fool. The kid who played Mercutio was a *freshman*."

I looked at Dad's face—he looked mad. "You know, Dad, the fact that you're still upset about this like twenty-five years later really isn't much comfort right now. I'm just gonna go to my room."

"Wait, wait! This story has an interesting postscript!" This is how Dad's stories always go. I really wish he'd try telling an interesting story with no postscript instead of a boring story with an interesting postscript, but he doesn't seem to have it in him.

"Go ahead." I sighed.

"So Jake is getting crazy phone numbers after every performance. From all the girls at our school, plus all these girls we've never even seen before. *College* girls. How many high school boys do you think get phone numbers from college girls? I'll tell you—it never happens. This was the only time in the history of the world it has ever happened. And there's me, just standing there, hoping maybe Jake will tell some of these girls he needs to double so I'll at least get a pity date out of the deal. Did I mention that I performed in a padded robe to make me look fat on top of everything else?"

"You didn't mention that."

"Yeah, well, I might as well have had a sign on that said NEVER DATE ME. Anyway, only one girl congratulated me on my performance. This really cute, shy girl from the basketball team came up to me blushing and said, 'You did a really good job.' And that, of course, was your mom."

I didn't really understand what the point was, but I didn't want to hurt his feelings, especially since he gets all sensitive when he's talking about Mom, the dead one, so I just let it go. "Thanks, Dad."

"Okay, sweetie. Life is tough, but you're tougher. Remember that." And suddenly he was hugging me and I was crying like a little girl.

"It's just so unfair. So unfair," I blubbered, and he rubbed my back and said, "I know, sweetie. I know."

5

Eventually I stopped crying and Dad gave me some Oreos and whatever milk was left after my idiot brothers had finished making udders out of latex gloves and milking them into their mouths.

I took my snack up to my room and flipped open my phone. The screen was black. I had turned it off at the beginning of practice because Geezer gave this speech on the first day about how you didn't disrespect the team by having your phone go off when you were supposed to be practicing. Like I had a lot of respect for the team at this point anyway.

I had eight texts from Lena. "R U mad?" "Pls call b4 I lose service," that kind of thing. Where Lena and her family go in New Hampshire there's no cell phone service, like it's 1870 or something.

I called her and she picked up on the first ring.

"Hey," she said. "Are you mad at me?"

"Of course not. I mean, I'm mad at Geezer, but not you."

"Geezer?"

"Conrad called her that."

"That's awesome. Wait. Did he say anything else?"

"Yeah, he told me how he pines for your love."

She was silent for a few seconds, and I felt bad for teasing her. "I'm joking, Lene."

"Oh yeah, I knew that. I mean, I don't think he'd really say 'pines.'"

"Not unless he was talking about trees."

Awkward silence fell. How weird was that? Usually the only awkwardness I felt while talking to Lena was how to get off the phone when I still had four hundred stupid things to say to her. Finally I bit the bullet. "So, uh, how was practice?"

"You are a way better goalie than that girl. She's only there because she's a senior."

"Yeah, that's what Conrad said."

"Was that before or after he talked about pining for my love?"

I laughed. "After. Of course the pining was the first thing he said to me."

"Damn right. Just tell him he's gonna have to get in line," she said.

"Okay," I said. Now she was the one making a joke that kind of hurt. Because of course Lena would have tons of guys lining up for her, probably even gorgeous Duncan, so hot that nobody ever even made the obvious donut joke about him, while I just stood to the side and passed out the numbers. We didn't say anything for a minute.

"Well, have a good weekend."

"Yeah, it's supposed to rain the whole time. We'll probably stay inside and play cards until we kill each other."

I laughed. "Make sure you're the one still standing at the
end. I'm not doing the first day of school without you."

"I know. Totally. I'm terrified. I'll call you when we get
back."

"Okay. Bye!" She didn't answer, and my phone said "call
was lost."

I texted Mom at work to tell her the bad news. I didn't
like to call her in case she was in a meeting or something. "I
got cut and Lena didn't," I wrote.

A couple of minutes later my phone beeped, and Mom
replied: "That sux. Ice cream tonite?"

See, now whereas Dad thinks boring me with some story
about how he was a loser is the way to react to something
like this, Mom knows exactly what you need when you're
upset.

"Totally," I texted back.

"Girls only," she replied. I flipped the phone closed and
smiled. I picked up my last summer reading book and tried to
read but couldn't because of the noise. All three boys were
now playing Mario Party, and I could hear Conrad bellowing
in his best Luigi voice, "Im-a De Best!"

I plugged my ears with my iPod and read for a while, but
a few minutes later Dominic came knocking at my door.

"Yeah?" I said, annoyed. Why wouldn't the kid let me sulk?

"Amanda?"

"Yeah."

"Will you play Operation with me?"

I took a moment before I answered. I really wanted to tell him to buzz off and go bug somebody else, but then I'd feel guilty and sad instead of just sad. I knew he was up here because Dad and Conrad never let him win at anything, and I always let him win. Well, I didn't have a choice.

"Sure. Come on in," I sighed.

He came in, all smiles, with the battered Operation box under his arm. "Great. Dad and Conrad are hogging the video games."

"Yeah, they'll do that," I said. We spent the next half hour digging plastic bits out of a two-dimensional guy. I like playing Operation with Dominic because it requires no effort at all to figure out how to let him win without looking like you're letting him win. Just pick up the water on the knee or whatever and buzz against the side and act mad.

Dominic was about a thousand dollars ahead of me when he suddenly busted out with "I hate school."

"How come?" I asked.

"Because it's boring and hard," he said.

"Yeah," I replied.

"I don't want to go," he whined.

"Me neither," I said.

"So why don't we stay home? We can homeschool ourselves! And take field trips and stuff."

It was weirdly appealing. Not so much the hanging out with my eight-year-old brother all day, though he had managed to make me forget how upset I was for a few minutes, but the idea of opting out of everything. No high school, no cliques, no popularity, no grade-grubbing, no scary new school, none of it. Just stay home and read and occasionally play soccer. I could see why people did it.

And yet, still. "I think I might miss Lena," I said.

"Yeah," he agreed. "You would."

I felt okay playing with Dominic, but as soon as Dad called out, "Dom! I've got to get dinner started if you want this controller!" he ran out of my room like he was shot out of a gun, and it only took about five seconds for me to start feeling really sorry for myself again.

Fortunately, Mom got home from work and came up to talk to me. "Hi there," she said. "I'm really sorry, honey."

"Thanks," I said.

"Do you want to talk about it?" she asked.

"Not really. I'm sorry. I just— I can't talk about it without crying, and I'm feeling kind of cried-out."

She put her hand on my shoulder, which is something she can only really do when I'm sitting and she's standing. "Okay. Hot fudge and mini M&M's after dinner?"

"Yeah," I said, and smiled.

Later, Dominic had a fit because Mom wouldn't let him squirt milk from a latex udder into his mouth at the dinner table, and then Dad got in trouble for letting him do it in the first place. I knew I wasn't the insane one.

Mom asked, "So, Conrad, how was your day?"

"Okay," he said, and then he reached into the pocket of his soccer shorts and pulled out a crumpled piece of paper. "You have to sign this."

Mom looked at the paper, all wrinkled and damp with

Conrad's butt sweat. I thought about offering her a latex glove, but she just said, "Okay, we'll deal with that later. What is it?"

"It's the no-booze pledge."

I had planned to give mine to Mom when Dad wasn't around. I was surprised at Conrad for making such a rookie mistake. "What the hell is that?" Dad asked. Conrad handed Dad the nasty piece of paper, and Dad smoothed it out on the table (ew!) and read aloud, "We, the undersigned, pledge that blank will not consume alcohol, marijuana, or any other controlled substance at any time during the academic year. We further understand that breaking this pledge will result in a two-game suspension for a first offense, and ineligibility to participate in athletics for the remainder of the academic year for a second offense."

Dad had his mad face on. "Well, this is just outrageous. We're not signing this."

Conrad said, "Dan"—he calls Dad "Dan," I guess out of loyalty to his biological dad—"I already signed it. Everybody and their parents have to sign it or you can't play sports."

"Why is this the first I've heard about this?"

Mom patted Dad's hand. "Because I signed it last year without telling you because I knew you'd make a big deal out of it."

"Um, I'm sorry," I added, "but why is this a big deal?"

Mom, Conrad, and Dominic all looked at me like I was a complete idiot for asking this question, which I guess I was.

"It's a big deal because it's an infringement on your rights.

Listen, I can see how they don't want you showing up drunk at practice or anything, but it's tying your private behavior off the field to your eligibility to play sports. I mean, doesn't that feel a little intrusive to you? Is there a chastity pledge we have to sign too? Surely if the school wants to have veto power over the private behavior of its students, there ought to be a chastity pledge here too. Or at least a condom-use pledge. I mean, it'll be taken just as seriously. Honestly, are you telling me that nobody from the football and hockey teams ever takes a drink during the school year? Have things changed that much since I was in high school? Conrad?"

Conrad was giggling. "No, sir, they have not."

"So by signing this, we're saying that the school can control your private behavior, and we're signing away your privacy essentially for nothing, because everyone understands that this is a sham document."

"Yeah, I guess that's pretty much it."

"What's a sham document?" Dominic asked.

"It's something like this," Dad said, holding Conrad's soggy form aloft.

"A sweaty piece of paper?" Dominic said, and everybody who wasn't Dad laughed, and Dad stopped talking, which was a relief.

I must be a glutton for punishment. While Mom was getting ready for our ice cream run after dinner, I decided to ask Dad about the form again because he was so mad. Since he was always telling us not to drink and stuff, I didn't really get it.

I found Dad in the living room. "So, Dad, I thought you didn't want us to drink."

He snapped his computer shut and said, "I don't, honey. But that's between us. The school has nothing to do with it. I just think the school is butting into your private life where it has no business. As long as you follow the rules while you're at school or participating in athletics, why should whatever else you do matter? I mean, it starts with something like this form, which everybody signs without thinking because who wants to look like they're standing up for teen drinking? But suppose the school wants to extend this to, like, I don't know, having a clean driving record. Or having sex before the legal age of consent. Is any of that stuff the school's business?"

"I guess not."

"Exactly. Which is why I'm calling the athletic director on Monday to talk about this."

Mom appeared at this point to inject some sanity into the conversation. "Dan, you're not doing any such thing. You'll humiliate the kids."

"By standing up for their rights?"

She looked at Dad like he was a total idiot. "Dan, were you ever a teenager? Would you have wanted your mom calling your high school about something like this?"

"Well, no, but . . ."

Mom gave him a kiss. "I love you to death, and I love your passion"—ew, even if she didn't mean it that way, not something I wanted to hear—"and your convictions, and it is important for the kids to know about the issues involved, but you do understand that their happiness and avoidance of humiliation is important. Right? Right?"

Dad blushed. "I don't know. I guess so."

Mom whispered something in his ear and he got this big smile on his face, which made me want to be somewhere else. Instead of fleeing, I cleared my throat, and Mom said, "Okay! Hot fudge and mini M&M's."

"Actually I changed my mind. I was thinking about Heath bars," I answered.

"See," Mom told Dad as we were leaving, "we like to debate important issues too!"

6

The long weekend totally sucked. Lena was gone and out of cell phone range, so me and my step half whatever siblings just sat around getting on each other's nerves, because I guess everybody was stressed about school. Well, Dominic was really stressed about school, anyway. Every night at bedtime he was crying about what if his friends weren't in his class, what if his teacher was mean, stuff like that. He got very wrapped up in the homeschool fantasy. I heard him yelling a couple of times, "Amanda can be my teacher!" No thank you.

I was actually more stressed out about soccer than school. I pretty much knew how to do school. Not to be too conceited, but I was good at it. Of course, I used to think I was good at soccer too, and I obviously wasn't.

Conrad didn't worry about anything, or if he did, he did a great job of hiding it. He just sat there playing video games while Dominic and I picked on each other. No, that's not true. Dominic made annoying noises and did all this stuff to get on my nerves, and I tried not to let it get to me, but eventually it would be too much, and I would scream at him and he would go crying to Mom, and I'd storm up to my room. Fun stuff!

Lena finally got back to civilization late Monday afternoon. After we'd established that both of our weekends sucked, we started talking about school.

"I'm totally freaking out," she panted.

"Yeah, me too," I said.

"What are you going to wear?"

"I've spent the last hour trying to figure out which of my new outfits makes me look the least hideous. So far each one makes me look hideous in a different way."

"Shut up. You're going to look great. Hey, can I bring my outfits over so we can help each other?"

I hesitated for a second, and then I instantly felt bad about it. "I . . . uh . . . yeah! Absolutely!" I felt awful inside. I couldn't believe I'd thought for even a second about telling her not to come over. Just because I was jealous of her body and, oh yeah, the whole soccer thing too. I was a horrible friend. If it had been me who made varsity and Lena who didn't (as if), I would be really hurt if she let something stupid like that come between us.

And yet it was coming between us. We had a good time trying on clothes—well, I let her convince me that I looked pretty in one of my outfits even though it was an obvious lie. I appreciated that she worked so hard at it.

But soccer was always there. We were obviously both thinking about it, but what could we say? Finally, after the third awkward silence, Lena was the one who had the guts to bring it up. Of course. Because she's a better friend than me on top of everything else.

"Keezer's a total witch," she said. "She was really mean in practice, yelling at everybody like they were total idiots."

What was I going to say? It's too bad you made varsity as a ninth grader? All I could think to say was "Well, Ms. Beasley's really nice. So at least there's that."

Lena just looked at me. "I'm sorry. It's so unfair."

"No, it's not. I mean, what's-her-name is a senior, and they can't carry me as a backup goalie if I can't run. It makes total sense."

"It's not as fun without you. I don't like it as much. It used to be fun, you know, and now it's only about winning, and who cares if it's any fun. I had three messages from her from over the weekend. Listen to this!"

Lena whipped out her cell phone, called her voice mail, and put it on speakerphone. "It's Saturday morning," Keezer's voice said out of the tinny little speaker, "and just because you can't practice with the team doesn't mean you can't practice. Make sure you run every day. Two miles is an okay number for a holiday weekend. You're fast, but you need to watch out for offsides. If you can get a three-on-three scrimmage together, you can practice offsides. Call me if you have questions."

I couldn't help laughing. "Did you call?"

"I was out of range, remember? Besides, she gave me detailed instructions on all these passing and shooting drills I could run too."

"Did you do any of this stuff?"

"I didn't get the messages until today. And anyway, it's not like I was going to run soccer drills inside the house in New Hampshire in the rain. She needs to relax."

"It sure sounds like it."

Lena went home after dinner. She had been really nice. So why did I feel so awful? I got the good coach, and she got the scary one.

Still, we were supposed to be complaining to each other about the coach, like we'd done before.

I moped around after dinner, flipping channels while Dad read, Conrad did whatever he did in his room, which is not something I want to think about, and Dominic had his nightly crying jag.

Mom came into the living room looking exasperated. "Amanda, he's asking for you. Will you go talk to him?"

"Uh, okay," I muttered as I headed upstairs. Dominic was sitting up in his bed in his SpongeBob pajamas looking pathetic. "Hey, buddy," I said. "What's up?"

"I don't want to go. It's too scary. Will you please stay home with me? Please?"

"Hmmm . . . how many times did I make you cry this weekend?"

"I don't know—five or six?"

"So basically twice a day. I don't think even a horrible teacher would make you cry that much. It's gonna be okay, you know? Conrad got through third grade, and you're way smarter than him."

"Really?"

"Really. Now try to get some sleep, okay?"

"Okay. Will you send Mommy back?"

"You got it."

I went back to the living room and told Mom she was wanted. "Your turn," she told Dad. "Go tell him a story or something."

Dad's face lit up and he headed upstairs. When I was sure he was out of earshot, I asked Mom, "What, are you trying to bore the kid into submission?"

Mom gave me this amused look and said, "He really needs to get to sleep. I figured I'd prescribe a sleep aid."

I continued to flip through channels, because everything on TV was annoying me. "So," Mom said after about five minutes, "do you think we could watch something else, or are you actually into that hunting knife show on the home shopping channel?"

I looked at the TV and some guy was holding up a big knife while an 800 number flashed on the bottom of the screen. "I don't care. You wanna watch something?" I handed Mom the remote.

"Nah." She turned the TV off. "Everything all set for tomorrow?"

Is everything all set? Nothing is set at all. Lena and I will be in separate homerooms and get separate schedules and I'm going to lose my best friend and my favorite sport and my life will be over.

"Yep!" I chirped. "I guess it is!"

Mom took a long look at me. Finally she said, "Okay," but she didn't sound convinced.

7

I don't remember my mom dying or anything, but I do kind of remember the time after she died and before Dad met Mom, just weird little snapshot memories of Dad crying hysterically and me getting freaked out because I was a little kid and crying hysterically was *my* job.

The one way in which Dad is right about the whole thing affecting me is that I never ever think, "Well, it can't get much worse." It can always get worse. It can get so much worse that somebody ends up dead.

So, knowing that, I wasn't too surprised when, on the first day of school, it got worse.

Dad wanted to take me to school, but fortunately Mom told him what I would have told him, which was that school was only a couple of blocks away, I could certainly walk there like Conrad did, and I had been going to the high school for soccer practice every day for the last two weeks.

Dad, unable to embarrass me in public, tried his best to

embarrass me in private. He gave me this big hug and held it too long, like I was going away for the year or something.

"Dad," I said, "you know, I am going to be back this afternoon after soccer practice."

"I know," he said. "Just give me a second here."

"Okay."

"This is a hard time for everybody," he whispered, "but remember—"

"I know, I know, tough as an old boot. I got it," I finished, and he laughed.

"Damn right. Now get the hell out of here."

Dad is so weird. Still, I guess in the end it's better to have this kind of dad than one of those guys who's always at work and figures he can't be in the same room as his daughter as soon as she starts wearing bras. Like Lena's dad, for example.

I got to school, and there were like a million kids there, and everybody was doing the hugging and squealing and oh-my-God-your-hair-looks-amazing-ing. Well, the girls were doing that. The guys were doing the arm-punching, shoulder-bumping, and "sup"-ing. Where was Lena?

I whipped out my phone to text her. There was no way I'd be able to hear her with all the squealing and "sup"-ing going on around me. "Where R U?" I sent.

"Btwn the Lions," she sent back, and I smiled. That was our favorite show when we met in the third grade. I headed for the steps that were guarded by the big stone lions, looking for Lena but having a hard time picking her out in the flood of humanity that was washing over the steps.

"Nice toothpicks!" I heard a guy say. I had almost convinced myself that this was not some jerk talking about my legs when I heard the same voice go "Oof! What the hell?" and then I heard Conrad's voice go "Say something else about my sister, asshole."

So I was actually being mocked for my freakish body on the first day of school. Fantastic. The fact that Conrad had stood up for me was nice, but it would have actually been nicer if he didn't have to. Oh well.

Finally I spotted Lena, an island of sanity in this horrible sea of people. Two really tall and really cute guys were talking to her, and she was doing this giggly flirty laugh that sounded nothing like her. I got up to them and she was like, "Oh, hey. Guys, this is my best friend, Amanda!"

I raised my hand in greeting and said, as brightly as I could manage, "Hey!"

"'Sup," they mumbled, and faded into the crowd.

Lena was beaming. "Wow!" she said. "The guys here are so nice!" Yeah, unless you've got toothpick legs. "Are you ready?"

"As ready as I'll ever be."

"Okay. Let's do it." And we walked into school together. We both had the letter with our homeroom assignments in our hands. I was in 319, she was in 348.

Strangely, these turned out to be right across the hall from each other, which was good because we could stand in the hall together being terrified until the bell rang. Well, I was terrified, anyway. I exchanged quiet greetings with the other JV girls I saw, and once in a while a junior or senior girl would walk by and greet Lena with a big hug or a hearty "Have a great day!"

This happened because the third floor, where our homerooms were, was also the home of the seniors' lockers and some of the juniors' lockers. I guess because somebody thought that having your locker and homeroom on the same floor might make your life too easy or something.

Finally the bell rang and we said goodbye and went into our homerooms. After the tedious business of calling everybody's name, my homeroom teacher, Mr. Knarr, an art teacher with a goofy smile, said, "Okay, I have a bunch of really boring stuff I'm supposed to read to you guys, but I'd just as soon skip that if it's all the same to you. You got the handbook mailed to your house, so I don't think we need to go over every single rule, right? And you've used combination locks before, right, so I don't need to go over that, though I probably should tell you that the school can cut your lock off and search your locker without cause at any time, so if you have any . . . interesting hobbies, you might not want to leave the evidence lying around in your locker."

The members of the Future Burnouts of America club laughed, and at that moment, somebody's cell phone went off. Okay, I had been mocked publicly and separated from my best friend and kicked off the good soccer team, but at least my phone didn't start playing a song from *High School Musical 3* in the middle of homeroom. So I guess it really could be worse.

The girl whose phone it was—this heavy, pale girl with frizzy, mousy hair—turned purple with embarrassment and started digging in her purse.

"Bless you!" Mr. Knarr said, and people smiled. "Those

fall allergies are killer. I too sound like Zac Efron when I sneeze." Everybody laughed, and the purple girl faded to red and looked like she wanted to disappear under her desk instead of die on the spot, so I guess he handled it pretty well.

"On an unrelated note, you may have read in the handbook the sensible and completely enforceable rule that cellular phones are not allowed in school and are subject to confiscation. The school cannot search your person without cause, though, so as long as your phones are invisible and set not to ring, the one or two of you who brought phones to school"—everybody laughed—"should be able to avoid getting in trouble.

"Now, for the moment you've all been waiting for. Your schedules." He handed everybody's out, then said, "After the name of the class is a one or two. One is for honors classes, two is for regular classes. Take a few minutes to ponder your schedules, and then we'll talk again."

I pondered mine. I couldn't help noticing the "2" after my math class. So that meant I was in "regular" math. Since, according to Conrad, something like 60 percent of the school is in honors classes, because that's just how special our beloved Charlesborough is, that meant I had basically been cut from the A team *again*.

"Those of you who are certain there's been a terrible mistake in your placement, put your complaint in writing, and I'll be sure to file it appropriately." Mr. Knarr held up the wastepaper basket when he said this. Did everybody on the staff here have, like, *1001 Corny Jokes for Teachers* or something? "No, I'm kidding. Go down and fight the crowds at guidance if you have questions. You'll probably have to make an appointment."

I fumed until the bell rang and we had time to go set up our lockers and go to guidance. I met Lena in the hall and looked at her schedule. We had the same classes, except, of course, for math, where she had level one and I had level two.

"Well, at least we've got everything else together," Lena said. "See?" She handed me her schedule.

"Yeah, that's—wait a minute. You're in English 9-1-B!"

"Um, yeah?"

"So I'm in English 9-1-A! We're not in the same English class!" In fact, we were in different sections for everything, no doubt because me being in bonehead math had messed up my schedule so I wouldn't be with Lena *at all*.

I figured I could set up my locker later, so I said goodbye to Lena and practically ran to guidance. One good thing was that I was able to talk to my guidance counselor right away. He was a tall, white-haired guy who was the boys' JV soccer coach, and somehow he knew I was Conrad's sister even though we have different last names.

"I'm really sorry, Amanda," he said. "I know this is hard. But the eighth grade teachers make the recommendations for leveling ninth graders, and the teachers will murder me if I mess with that stuff. If they've made a terrible mistake, your math teacher will see that, and you can move up."

It turned out that Mr. Blair, my eighth grade Algebra teacher, was evil as well as boring. Of course I hadn't done well in his class! He was the most boring person on the face of the earth, and he spoke in a monotone all the time. How can you possibly pay attention to somebody droning on and on at 7:40 in the morning?

I really wanted to cry, but I pushed my tears back inside and made them stay there and was determined to walk through this horrible day in this horrible school with my head held high.

I heard Dad's voice in my head again. "Tough as an old boot," he whispered.

Yeah, Dad, but if I'm the old boot, why am I the one who keeps getting kicked?

8

Back in middle school, lunch with Lena always helped me get through a stressful day. Like pretty much whatever was going on, she could get me to laugh about it. And that's the way lunch started today.

"Oh my God, this math class is going to kill me," I said. "It's me and a bunch of burnouts and poor Nick Randall. I mean, the kid is nice, but he's dumb as a doorknob, and I'm in class with him!"

"Too bad you don't sell weed," she answered.

"What the hell are you talking about?"

"Well, burnouts with bad math skills—it seems like an awesome moneymaking opportunity. You could totally cheat them and they'd probably thank you for it!"

I was upset, but I couldn't help laughing, picturing me in the back of the room with baggies and a scale and everything, as if that would ever happen. I'd be more likely to start shopping in petites. "I think I'll probably go for the job over at the ice cream shop, if it's all the same to you."

"Yeah, I don't know how often my mom would let me visit you in jail."

"It might solve my problem of never having anything to wear though." Yes, my fashion problem is so bad I was actually pondering the positives of prison uniforms.

"Don't go to jail for fashion," Lena said. "I'm sure we can get you some manly blue work shirts here on the outside if you decide that's a look you want."

Okay, I was starting to feel better. Even talking about stupid stuff with Lena made me feel better. But then a couple of varsity girls stopped by where we were sitting.

"Hey, Lena," they said, smiling.

"Oh, hey!" Lena chirped. "Mo, Lauren, this is Amanda. You remember her from practice?"

"Oh yeah," one of them said. "Hey."

"How's your first day?" the other one said to Lena, and Lena started talking about how totally awesome everything was, and pretty soon a couple more girls stopped by the table, and it wasn't long after that that a few guys stopped by. And not just any guys. Older guys. Soccer-playing guys. Guys including Duncan, the hottest guy in school. Really cute guys. Tall guys. Guys who had no business even looking at somebody five feet four inches tall because they could find a nice tall girl more appropriate for someone of their height sitting right next to her.

In a way I guess it was for the best that I turned invisible to everyone, because if Duncan had acknowledged my existence at all, I would have sputtered and stammered and generally acted like an idiot.

I had kind of expected to be invisible to the varsity girls because of my lowly JV status, and I was used to being invisible to guys like Duncan or pretty much anyone else for that matter, but not to Lena. When I got up to throw away my trash, she was deep in conversation with Brandi or Courtney or somebody. Anyway, a beautiful girl with long blond hair and a cute boyfriend hanging all over her.

The afternoon was not marred by any bad math classes, so it was actually an improvement over the morning, even though I was still stung by being ignored by my best friend. The very worst part of the whole thing was trying to picture the situation reversed. Would I be a strong enough person to say, "Hey, popular girls and cute boys, please include my invisible friend in the conversation! I hate being the center of attention! I refuse to vault several steps up the social ladder in my new school!" Of course I wouldn't. In a way, then, I was only getting what I deserved. How could I expect Lena to be a better friend than I would be in this situation? It was like I was being punished for wanting the attention by having to watch her get it.

In English class, the teacher—a short guy who seemed to think that our being nervous about school was hilarious—announced that we'd be starting with poetry. He split us into groups to talk about this poem called "To an Athlete Dying Young."

I was in a group with Sarah Kestrel, who I knew from fifth grade and liked okay; Tom Castor, who I knew from alphabetical order in middle school; and some guy I didn't know named Angus. I swear to God. Like the beef.

"I think," Tom said, "that the poem is saying it's kind of cool that he died young because he'll never see his record broken."

"Yeah," Sarah agreed. "It's a romantic idea."

"I think it's a dumb idea," I said. I thought it was dumb because it seemed to be saying that if you were a great athlete in your teens, it wouldn't matter when you got old. I mean, so what if Lena wouldn't be a great soccer player at forty-five? At least she was once! And was that how long I'd have to wait to step out of her shadow?

"It's a completely stupid poem," Angus growled, and his face was getting red. "It's just about the single stupidest thing I've ever read."

Everybody paused for a moment, and then I joked, "Well, you obviously didn't read *A Separate Peace* over the summer like we were supposed to," and, at the same time, Sarah said, "Whoa. Somebody's a little touchy."

Angus smiled at me and glared at Sarah. "If you've seen somebody die young, you know there's nothing good about it. This guy is a total idiot. Like you should kill yourself as soon as you win a race, because it's all downhill from there, and there's nothing else worth living for."

"Uh," Tom offered, "I don't really see anything in here about killing yourself."

At that point the teacher, Mr. Gordon, interrupted us, and each group had to report to the big group. It wasn't clear what the point of the whole thing was, but it was cool to at least get to talk about our opinions for once instead of just writing down the teacher's.

I don't know what made me do this, but after class as we were packing up our stuff, I said to Angus, "Hey, I'm sorry."

"For what?" he said. His face was red like he was still upset.

"About whoever died young."

His face softened a little bit, and he whispered, "Thanks."

"My mom died," I said. "When I was little, I mean. I don't really remember." Now why did I say that? Our family status is so weird and complicated that I usually avoid saying anything that will make me have to explain it all.

"I'm sorry," Angus answered. "It's . . . sometimes it's worse to remember." We both stood there not talking until Angus added, "Well, see ya," and bolted from the room.

After I got rid of my books, I headed to the locker room to get ready for soccer practice.

Lena was there, and she asked, "Hey, Manda, what happened to you at lunch?"

"I guess I disappeared," I answered without looking at her. I needed to get out on the field and focus on stopping balls and not think about anything else right now. I opened a locker and took off my shirt and shoved it in there, pulling on my SOCCER IS LIFE! T-shirt and then wishing I'd brought another one because Lena and I bought those matching shirts at the mall at the beginning of summer, also known as a lifetime ago.

"Are you mad at me or something?" Lena asked.

"Why would I be mad? Just because you ignored me for a bunch of people you just met? Why would I be mad about that?"

"Oh my God, Amanda, we were having a conversation, and I just turned to say hi to some people, and then you were gone."

"You didn't just turn to say hi to them," I whisper-yelled at her. The older girls were filtering into the locker room, and I didn't want to have a big fight in front of everybody and be the subject of all kinds of gossip. "You joined their conversation and I sat there for *eight minutes* while you didn't say a *word* to me, and finally I left."

Lena looked at me for a second like she was going to yell at me, but then my best friend swam up through the sea of Lena's new popularity and showed her face to me again. "Eight minutes? Really?"

"I . . . uh . . . I timed it." I flashed my digital sports watch with the heart rate monitor that I'd gotten for my last birthday at her.

Lena looked at the floor. "Wow," she whispered in the direction of her cleats. "That was bitchy. I'm sorry."

"It's okay," I answered.

"No, it's not. I'd be totally pissed if you did that to me. I won't do that again," she promised.

"Cool then."

"Friends?"

"To the end," I said, and extended a hand. She clasped it, and it was funny how that one moment seemed to turn my whole day around.

And then practice was awesome. Mostly. We did the usual drills, and we scrimmaged, and my team won 3–2, not that I was keeping track of the score in a scrimmage. One of the goals against me was this amazing lucky shot right up in the corner of the goal that no human goalie could have possibly stopped, so I didn't feel too bad about that, but the other one I just guessed wrong and went the wrong way with my hands and watched as the ball sailed past my feet and into the goal.

"Nice job," Ms. Beasley told me at the end of the scrimmage.

"I should have had that second goal," I replied.

"Well, I think Kate accidentally deked you."

"What do you mean?"

"I mean, the boys' team was practicing over to the left, and somebody obviously has a crush, so she was distracted and you saw her eyes going that way and thought that's the way the ball was going. Don't watch the eyes. Watch the feet." She clapped her hand on my shoulder, and I felt better. For a minute.

Then Beasley—somebody dropped the "Ms." at the beginning of practice and she rolled her eyes and smiled, so after that it would have suddenly seemed really uncool to call her Ms. Beasley—called us together.

"Okay," she announced. "Tomorrow is our first game, and I want you to do your best, but I don't want anyone to freak out. I want to see you using what you've learned, but this is not the win-at-all-costs team. Don't get me wrong— it's more fun to win than it is to lose, but that's the reason to win—because it's more fun. Teams almost never go undefeated, and we are going to lose some games. Which is fine, because you probably learn more from your losses than your victories. We're going to play everyone in the conference twice, so what I'd really like to see is you showing that you've learned something the second time we play a team. You'll know which players are dirty, which ones you should double, stuff like that.

"In any case, you've been working really hard, and I'm sure we're going to do well tomorrow."

We started to get up, but then this red-haired senior with one jet-black streak in her hair and a CHILD SOLDIERS RUN AMOK shirt on walked over from the field hockey field, and Beasley said, "Hang on, girls. Two more things. One is, well, here's Rosalind."

Rosalind, the senior with red hair, smiled at us. "Hey, guys. I just want to let you know that my stepmom runs the Charlesborough Yoga Studio over in Curley Square, and she gives deep discounts to Charlesborough athletes. So if you tell them at the desk that you play CHS soccer, you'll get any class for half price. It helps a ton with your flexibility, preventing injury, stuff like that. Maybe I'll see you there sometime!"

She waved her stick at us and ran back to the field hockey field, and I totally wanted to be her. She was confident and pretty and nice and looked like she had never felt unsure of herself or uncomfortable in her own skin or any of the things I felt all the time.

"I know you guys are busy, but I was injured constantly until I started doing yoga my sophomore year in college," Beasley told us.

"You played in college?" somebody asked.

"Yeah," Beasley said.

"Were you any good, Beasley?"

"I don't know . . . I guess so."

"Like how good were you?"

"My senior year I was the eighth alternate for the national team," Beasley practically whispered, her face bright red.

"So you were the twenty-ninth-best player in the United States?" I said, and then I was immediately embarrassed, but apparently not as embarrassed as Beasley was.

"I don't know . . ." Beasley offered, and then everybody was talking at once. How cool was that? Our soccer coach was in the top thirty players in the whole country! There's no way Geezer was ever that good at anything.

"Why'd you stop?" I asked, and the whole team fell silent.

"Well, Amanda, it's a long story, but the short version is that, no matter what your shirt says, soccer isn't life. It's really fun and beautiful and cool, but there are other things in life that are fun and beautiful and cool, and if you want to play soccer at that level, you have to give up a lot of the other fun, beautiful, and cool things."

I realized I was going to have to chew on that idea for a while. Since pretty much everything that was beautiful and fun and cool in my life came from playing soccer, it was hard to imagine anything else.

"But enough about me," Beasley said. "Let's talk about you. Now you know our games are always going to take place before the varsity games, against the same schools and on the same fields. So unless I get a specific written excuse from your parents saying that you have a medical appointment or a funeral to attend, I expect you to stick around and watch every varsity game."

We all made a shocked, unhappy noise at this, and Beasley just raised her voice over us and kept talking. "There are two reasons for this. One is that it's simply the right thing to do to support girls' soccer. You guys know that compared to football or basketball games, our games are not going to draw big crowds. At some of the away games it is possible that you'll be the only people there supporting varsity, and so you need to do it. Period.

"The second reason is that you can learn a lot from watching these games. You can really dissect what's going on in the game when you're not under the pressure of playing it, and that's going to make you better players. Not to mention that you will all be varsity players sooner or later, and so you should see the kind of system that Coach Keezer runs. Also, you'll be playing against some of the same girls next year and the year after, so if you've seen their games, you'll have a leg up when you do get on varsity. I know none of you are actually going to do this, but it would be a great idea to keep a notebook on what you see."

We sat in grumpy silence for a minute, probably thinking about how we'd have even less time to do homework on game days now. Finally, Shakina Williams, who was a pretty good forward, said, "So does that mean that varsity will be supporting us at all our games?"

"Well," Beasley stammered, "since we can only get the half buses, we have to travel separately, and the schedule—"

"So basically no, is what you're saying."

"Well, some of them will be there sometimes. I guess that's the best I can offer you."

"But," Fiona Goldberg objected, "isn't it simply the right thing to do?"

Beasley looked up to the sky like she thought it might tell her whether she should say something bad about Geezer. I held my breath, hoping that one of those moments where teachers dish on each other was coming.

"Girls," she said, "if you wait for everyone else to do the right thing before you do the right thing, then you'll never do what's right. You have to do what's right even if other people aren't. Maybe even especially if other people aren't."

Nobody spoke for a minute until Shakina yelled out, "Beasley's droppin' the wisdom!" That broke the tension. Everybody laughed, and Beasley said, "Okay, get outta here. And get a good night's sleep tonight!"

Soccer Season

1

I did not get a good night's sleep that night. It was a weird feeling: I was lying in bed with my eyes closed and everything, but it felt like I had forgotten how to fall asleep. Sometimes my heels hurt at night after I've been running really hard, which I can usually ignore enough to fall asleep, but not when my mind is in overdrive. The longer I lay there, the more my heels seemed to hurt, and the more times I looked at the clock, the more stressed I got about not being asleep, and the more hyper and awake I became.

I felt really angry and alone. I was sure pretty much everybody else in the house was asleep (because Mom and Dad go right to sleep as soon as they go into their room and shut the door, and they always have, no matter what the evidence named Dominic suggests). When I got up and looked out my window at the dark street with those sickly yellow puddles of light from the streetlights, it seemed like everybody else in the world was asleep too.

I decided to go watch some TV for a while. Maybe that would clear my head. I shuffled downstairs and found the TV already on. Dad was sitting on the couch, and he looked surprised when he saw me.

"Oh, hell," he said. "Welcome to the club."

"Dad, you're so random. What are you talking about?"

"Let me guess: you were lying there in bed with thoughts racing through your mind, and you felt like you forgot how to fall asleep. Like there was some switch in your brain that turned it all off, and you just forgot where it was."

I hadn't thought of the part about the switch, but it was actually a pretty good description of what I'd been feeling. "Yeah."

"Well, I'm sorry. Bad genes. Insomnia, I'm afraid, runs in the family. Which is why I'm sitting here watching *Satan's Cheerleaders* at one a.m."

"Is it any good?"

"It's way worse than any movie with that name should be. It's got Yvonne De Carlo, and you know, I always had a crush on her when she was Lily Munster—"

"Dad, TMI."

"Well, anyway, check her out."

I looked at the TV. "You had a crush on the old lady?"

"When she was . . . forget it."

We sat in silence watching the crappy movie for a few minutes. I could tell Dad was dying to say something, so finally I barked "What?" at him.

"I want to give you some advice, and I know it's going to be hard to take, but I just want you to listen."

"Okay."

"Sometimes you won't be able to sleep. And that sucks, but the only thing you can do to make it suck less is to just accept it. There are worse things in the world than being tired, and that's the worst that can happen. The more you stress about why this shouldn't be happening, the worse it'll be."

"But I have a game tomorrow."

"And you'll be so high on adrenaline that you'll probably play great and then come home and collapse. And the good thing is, if you're tired tomorrow, it will mellow you out a little bit and keep you from stressing all day."

"I hope so," I said, and turned my attention back to the movie. It must have been really crappy, because the next thing I knew, Lena and Courtney from varsity were laughing and punching me really hard in the stomach.

"What the hell!" I yelled. I opened my eyes and found myself on the couch with Dominic, clad in his SpongeBob pajamas, jumping up and plopping his butt onto my stomach.

I was awake in an instant. "You little monster! I'm gonna wake you up tomorrow pouncing on your guts. You freak! What is wrong with you?"

Dominic, manipulative little monster that he is, turned on the waterworks at this and went crying to Mom and Dad's room.

"Amanda!" Mom called down.

"What?" I called back up.

"I need to speak to you."

I trudged up the stairs thinking about how I was going

to go into Dominic's room after he fell asleep tonight and pounce on his guts and hopefully make him spew all over the place.

I got up to Mom and Dad's room, where the scene didn't look good. There was Dominic, red-faced and crying, snuggled into the crook of Dad's arm while Mom looked at me.

"Well?" she asked.

"I couldn't sleep last night and got up and fell asleep on the couch, and the next thing I knew, some freak in Sponge-Bob pajamas was bouncing up and down on my stomach."

"Amanda. That's it for the name-calling. You dehumanize people when you call them names."

"Yeah, well, they have to be human in the first place for that to work," I said, and Mom gave me the Look of Death and I shut up.

"Now, Dominic, you didn't tell us the part about jumping on Amanda's stomach while she was asleep. How do you think that made her feel?"

I rolled my eyes and walked away before Mom could extract an insincere apology from the little twerp and before I'd be called on to give an insincere apology of my own.

But then, forty-five minutes later, as I was running out the door, Dominic came up to me without Mom shoving him in my direction and, looking at the floor, he mumbled, "I'm sorry I jumped on your stomach."

And now I saw that he was a goofy kid and not some demon from hell sent to make my miserable life more miserable, so I just kind of tousled his hair and said, "I'm sorry I called you a freak."

"It's okay," he said.

"All right then, buddy," I said. "You gonna come to my game today?"

"Yeah!" he yelled, his face bright. I have to say this: the kid was my number one fan.

"I'll see you then," I said. I called goodbye to everybody else but Conrad, who was still in the shower because he was obviously planning on being late, and left for school.

On my walk, I couldn't help thinking that if yesterday sucked and it didn't start with somebody slamming sixty pounds into my stomach, how horrible was today going to be?

As it turned out, less horrible than I feared. Maybe it was because, like Dad said, I was tired and felt kind of dazed all day. So classes came and went and I didn't even really notice. At lunch, Lena didn't have time for me again, but at least this time she kept turning back to me and going, "What do you think, Amanda?" Which was still not enough to get Duncan to pull his eyes away from her, but that was okay because I was too tired at that point to charm him with my sparkling wit anyway.

Maybe this was my big opportunity to get in with this group, but I was too tired to make interesting conversation.

And, anyway, I wasn't sure I wanted to get in with this group. At least not as Lena's sidekick, which was all I would ever be to them. I didn't want to be popular with a bunch of kids I didn't even know. What I wanted was for things to be like they used to be, where it was Lena and me together against the world. Even with her remembering I existed, it still wasn't like it used to be. I wanted them all to go away, even the cute boys, so I could have my best friend back.

2

Our game was at home, and so Lena, who knew I was completely exhausted, went over to the store across the street after school and bought me an energy drink. I didn't know how drinking a barrel of sugar and caffeine would affect my sleep tonight, and I didn't really care. I had a game to play.

Lena sat with Dominic and Dad. Mom had apologized for not being able to get off work early enough, which was fine. It's weird, because of course both my parents are corny and embarrassing, especially Dad, but I always appreciate a parental representative in the stands at my games.

Lena was the only member of the varsity who showed up to watch our game. "I see your friend's the only one doing the right thing," Shakina observed before the game started.

"Yeah."

"Well, what do you say we put on a show for her? Maybe she'll tell the rest of them to come next time."

I answered "Yeah!" maybe a little too loudly, because

Shakina looked kind of embarrassed and everybody on the field looked at me. "Uh, too much caffeine, I guess."

In the first half, we did put on a show. The other team only got three shots on goal, and I stopped all of them easily, even the one that was perfectly placed right in the corner of the goal. We were up 2–0 at the end of the first half, and I felt great.

And then, in the second half, our offense collapsed, or else their offense woke up, but in any case, pretty much the whole half was played on our side of the field, and the shots just kept coming. My caffeine buzz from the gross orange drink was starting to wear off in a major way, and I felt a little sluggish. Even so, I managed to make four saves, including one penalty shot after Marcia got called for a totally unintentional handball in the box.

So any game where you stop a penalty shot is a good one, right? Well, it would have been except that I let in two goals in between my four saves, and I guess I lost a step or something by the end of the game, because we lost when the other team got this incredibly cheap goal on a weak shot that came limping out of a crowd of players in front of the goal. I should have seen it sooner, and even seeing it late, I should have been able to get to it. And might have if I'd been more awake.

When the game ended, I sat in the goal with my head in my hands. I couldn't sleep at least partly because I was nervous about soccer, and the lack of sleep that came from being nervous about soccer had made me suck at soccer. It was like stuff just kept piling on.

I had really wanted to prove that a mistake had been

made, that I belonged on varsity. Not that I thought they'd move me up, but I wanted Geezer to see how good I was and know that she'd screwed up. Instead, all I'd done was confirm her belief that I wasn't ready for varsity.

Well, the good news was that Geezer hadn't watched our game anyway. "Amanda," Beasley commanded, "get up and congratulate the other team."

This was always the worst part about losing—like it wasn't bad enough to get beaten, you had to go up to the people who'd made you look stupid and *thank them* for it.

I could tell from the look on Beasley's face that I'd hear a speech about how I'd be cooling my aching heels on the bench if I couldn't conduct myself like a good sport, so I got up, got in line, and slapped the hand of every girl on the other team, muttering, "Good game," even to the girl whose penalty shot I'd stopped, who greeted me with a friendly "You suck."

Still stinking of sweat and failure, we dutifully trooped into the bleachers with Beasley to cheer on varsity. I didn't want to look like too much of a brownnoser, but I had actually brought a notebook and a pen in my soccer bag. I looked around to see if anybody else was taking notes. They weren't, so the notebook and pen stayed in my bag.

We cheered for the varsity. I know this is bad, but I did enjoy the fact that the varsity goalie had a worse game than I did. By halftime it was tied 2–2, but really they should have been up 2–0, because both of the other team's goals were cheapies that could and should have been stopped.

Lena hadn't started, but they brought her in for the second half and she set the team on fire. I was proud to be her best friend. You could see the hate in the other team's eyes, because they had been paying attention to Courtney the whole first half and ignoring the wing, and now every time they turned around, Lena was streaking up the wing and crossing to Courtney in the center. They couldn't take the ball from her and they couldn't catch her—all they could hope to do was intercept the cross or stop the shot. (Which they actually could do from time to time because their goalie, unlike ours, could actually play.)

The final score was 5–4. We cheered our lungs out, and it was fun, though it didn't do much to take the sting out of our own humiliating defeat. It was also sort of painful to me, because I knew that, even with the horrible game I'd had, the margin of victory would have been bigger if I'd been in the goal. It was great that they'd scored five goals, but if you need five goals to win, you're in trouble because most teams won't let you have that many.

Unless you've got Lena on the wing with fresh legs in the second half. Then maybe every team will give up five goals or more.

One thing did make me glad I wasn't on varsity, though. We knew this from practice, but Geezer was a screamer. She spent the whole game screaming at her players for every mistake they made, and we never once saw her crack a smile or compliment anything anyone did right.

When the game ended, we could hear Geezer berating the team from way up in the bleachers.

"What do you think she does when they lose?" Shakina asked.

We all shook our heads like we didn't want to know.

As we were gathering up our stuff to go, Beasley said, "Amanda, can I talk to you for a second?"

Uh-oh. She'd waited for a whole other game to end before doing it, but now she was going to drop the bomb on me for my horrible performance. "Yeah?"

"Well, two things. One is that you played a really good game. Don't let one mistake make you think otherwise."

"But—"

"Expert talking here, okay? I did not see one player on any team today who had a perfect game." Really? Because it sure looked to me like Lena did.

"Okay."

"The other thing is that I did some research on Sever's disease."

"Yeah?"

"Yeah, and you should consider taking Rosalind up on that yoga thing. I really think it will help you."

"Okay. I guess I'll try it."

"Great. I'll see you tomorrow."

"Yes you will."

I tried not to sulk too much at home, but it was hard. Lena called, and two weird things happened. The first one was that she did not mention Conrad once. She usually managed to make some fake-casual question about him within the first thirty seconds of our call, but she didn't mention him at all this time. The other thing was that instead of our usual marathon conversation, we were only on the phone for a few minutes—okay, twenty, but still—when she got another call and said she had to go and she'd call me back. Who was more important than me? Well, I never found out because she never called me back.

Dad looked like he wanted to say something to me a couple of times, but Mom gave him this look that shut him up, and I was glad. She knew that there was nothing anybody could say that wouldn't make me feel horrible, so nobody said anything.

Well, I guess I should say there was nothing either of my parents could say to make me feel better because at dinner, Dominic said, "That was awesome the way you stopped that penalty kick! Nobody ever gets those!" And that did make me feel better—even if I'd muffed an easy shot, I'd gobbled up a nearly impossible one.

I did homework. Lena still didn't call back. I thought about calling her and asking since when did she not call me back, but I decided she was going to have to come to me. I was sick of thinking about stuff that made me sad, so I got online and looked up the schedule for Charlesborough Yoga Studio.

Mom came and snooped over my shoulder like she always does when I'm online, I guess to check that I'm not chatting with some creepy pedophile or something.

"Whatcha doing?" she asked, all fake casual.

"Oh. Well, we get half-price classes at this yoga studio, and Ms. Beasley told me she thought it would be a good idea for me to do it, so I figured I would take one class to see what it was like."

Mom stared at me for a minute and then said, "Who are you, and what have you done with my daughter?"

"What?"

"I have been trying to get you to go to yoga with me ever since you got your diagnosis. And you always made fun of me with all kinds of stuff about tight clothes and how you weren't going to go imitate a dog and how the whole thing was the stupidest, corniest thing you could even imagine. Does any of this ring a bell?"

It did. Slightly. My memory was that after I stopped doing the stupid stretching exercises that didn't help my Sever's disease at all, Mom suggested I take yoga and I said I was too busy. But I did think those things about the clothes and the dogs and the corniness, so unless Mom had read my mind, I must have actually said them.

"Well, Mom, you know, high school is a time of transition, and—"

She laughed. "I'm gonna call Ms. Beasley and have her tell you you'll play better if you clean your room."

She walked away shaking her head, and I called after her, "So can you take me to this seven o'clock class tomorrow night?"

I could hear the amusement fighting with the annoyance in her voice as she called out, "Yes, of course!"

3

They ought to give grades for lunch. I mean, if you think about it, it's the part of the day that requires the most knowledge and the most thinking. You have to understand all the rules about who sits where, even though nobody has ever written them down and nobody explains them. So every day is a high-stakes test, especially when somebody changes one of the factors you've come to take for granted.

Take today, when I went to lunch ready to sit with Lena, even though I still hadn't heard from her since she lied about calling me right back last night. I had dropped my folder on the way out of history class, and the time it took me to pick my papers up and put them away had made me late enough to lunch that Lena was already deep in conversation with Courtney when I got to the cafeteria.

Shakina and Marcia waved to me from their table. I stood there like an idiot for a minute. Lena still hadn't seen me, but either way this was a bad choice. I could go and sit with Lena and be a good friend and be mostly ignored and feel like a loser, or I could go and have a nice conversation with Shakina and Marcia and have a better lunch experience but look like a bad friend.

I decided to be a bad friend when Duncan went and started hovering around Lena yet again. No wonder she wasn't asking me about Conrad anymore. I didn't want to spend the whole lunchtime seething about how the guy I'd been nursing a secret crush on since mid-August when soccer practice started, a guy who was not only gorgeous but also taller than me, had also decided to pick Lena and cut me from the dating varsity. Well, I suppose he would have had to notice me in order to cut me, but still.

So I went and sat with Marcia and Shakina and talked and laughed and made myself not look over to where Duncan was drooling over Lena and not get jealous and not care.

On the way out of lunch, I saw a bunch of dorky boys I knew sitting at a table being goofy. I swear, they acted more like Dominic than like me, even though we were the same age. Down at the far end of their table, eating by himself, was Angus Beef from English class, reading a book. I'd had to make a hard choice, but at least I had two tables to choose from. How much must it suck to have nobody to sit with at all, to have your only option be to sit alone, excluded even from the group of boys making fart sounds? Angus looked up at me and waved, and I waved back. "Whatcha reading?" I asked.

He held up the book. *Animal Liberation*. I had no idea what it was. "Any good?"

"I'm not sure I agree with the whole thing, but it definitely makes you think," he said.

I had nothing to add to that. "See you in class then."

"Cool," he said, and buried his head back in the book. Well, at least he didn't seem to mind his social outcast status. He may have even chosen it. Weird.

I went to my locker to get my stuff for English, and Lena stopped by. "Hey! Where were you?" she asked.

"Hey, yourself," I said, trying to sound more casual than I felt. "How come you never called me back last night?"

"Oh my God, I am so sorry. Courtney was breaking up with Jonathan, and I had to hear all about it and she wouldn't let me off the phone until like nine-thirty, and then Mom told me it was too late to be on the phone and blah blah. Were you avoiding me because you're mad?"

"Oh no," I lied. "Not at all. Marcia was feeling really bad about the handball yesterday, and she stopped me to apologize, and she was being kinda high-maintenance, and it took me five minutes to convince her that it wasn't a big deal, and by that time I was already sitting there. Besides, it looked like you had somebody better-looking to talk to."

"Amanda, Courtney is not better-looking than you."

"I'm not talking about Courtney," I said, smiling.

Lena broke into this great big grin. "Is he the cutest thing on the face of the earth? It hurts my eyes to look at him. Too bad he likes Courtney."

"No way, he totally likes you."

"You're crazy!"

"No, I could read the body language from across the caf." True. I read his body language during lunch when I was not looking over there and not getting jealous. "It's all about you."

"His friend Jared is having a party on Saturday and he asked us to go, but I thought he was just being polite and asking me because I was sitting there. Oh my God, you have to come with me. I mean, I wasn't even going to go, but you have to go with me. I'm freaking out."

I patted her on the shoulder. "Don't freak out. Of course I'll go with you."

Of course. Because Mom and Dad will be delighted with the idea of me going to a kegger. Because I'd love to stand there feeling awkward while Captain Gorgeous hits on my best friend! Being a good friend completely sucks sometimes.

I was the first one at soccer practice that afternoon, and when I went to grab a ball, Beasley told me, "Grab a seat there first, Amanda. And don't sit on the ball. I hate it when people do that."

"What's up?" I asked nervously.

"You'll see," she said.

Everybody looked at me when they came to practice, and I just shrugged. Finally, when everybody was there, Beasley said, "Okay. Who can tell me something they learned from watching the varsity game yesterday?"

All the girls looked at each other. I guess we were

expecting her to go over what happened in our game. Finally I raised my hand.

"Amanda?"

"Well, I saw how important subs can be. The other team thought they had the offense figured out, but the offense totally changed when Lena came in the game. It took them two goals and a lot of yelling from their coach before they stopped marking Courtney and started paying attention to Lena."

"For all the good it did them," Beasley joked. "Great, Amanda. You've just earned your starting spot in the next game."

A lot of girls gasped when she said this. She'd told us to bring notebooks, but if anybody besides me had brought them, nobody had used them, and now she was giving out the starting positions based on who had something to say about the varsity game! I was really glad I went first because I didn't have much else to say.

"I told you I wanted you paying attention to what was happening in the varsity games. You'll be earning your starting positions for every game by showing that you're not just playing the game, you're studying it and trying to get better. Now, who's next?"

It took an agonizing twenty minutes for ten girls to come up with stuff to say, and so we spent a shorter time running around than usual, but I'd never spent so much time analyzing a soccer game before.

That night, getting ready to leave for yoga class, I was feeling uncomfortable about the whole thing. I was afraid I wasn't going to know what to do and everybody was going to make fun of me. Plus I had these tight leggings on.

"Do you have enough water?" Mom asked.

"Why do I need water to stretch?" I said.

"Didn't you say this was a hot yoga class?"

"Yeah," I answered. "But I thought that just meant hot like cool, like hey, this class is hot, it's got it goin' on, it'll make you really hot, they play hot jams on the stereo, something like that."

Mom actually laughed at me. "No, sweetie. It means it's going to be ninety-five degrees in the yoga studio."

"What!? Who thought of this? That's the dumbest thing I ever heard. No way am I going to go stretch in a sauna!"

"Well, I guess you'll have to tell Coach Beasley that you were scared—"

"I'm not scared, okay? It just seems bizarre. But fine, I'll try it."

So I filled up two water bottles, and when I walked into Charlesborough Yoga Studio, I told the lady behind the counter that I played CHS soccer.

She smiled and asked me for seven bucks, then directed me to the classroom.

I looked around the class, and it was all women Mom's age, plus a few guys, and then me in the back slowly unrolling the purple yoga mat Mom had given me.

I was totally embarrassed, but then Shakina came in looking just as scared and uncomfortable as I felt, and she ran over and unrolled her mat next to mine.

I didn't know how I was going to break this to Mom, but the class was awesome. The heat made my muscles that were always so tight feel like they'd melted into these wonderful flexible bands of goo.

And the instructor was tall. I estimated her height at five feet ten inches, same as me, and she had these skinny legs and practically no boobs, and she was beautiful. She looked so confident and so comfortable in her body, and she looked great because of that confidence she gave off. If that's what yoga does for you, I thought, I'm in.

Plus I had a great time with Shakina. We both screwed up all the time, and the instructor, whose name was Portia, kept coming over and correcting our form and being encouraging, and then when she left, Shakina and I would giggle about how bad we sucked at yoga.

Of course, there was the kind of dorkified stuff about saluting the sun and listening to your breath and all that stuff. I guess you were supposed to turn off your brain and not think about how freaking hot it was or how unflexible you were or the easy goal that you should have saved. Mostly it didn't work because my brain is always running through all this stuff at like a mile a minute, but right around the hour mark of the ninety-minute class, just for a second, it did work. I was bent into an impossible position with sweat pouring off me, and I was breathing, and I wasn't thinking. Even when the motor of my brain started up again, I felt this incredible relief. My brain was overjoyed to get a break from running on the treadmill of my thoughts. It felt great, and I wanted more. More than my heels not hurting, more than my legs feeling soft and flexible, more than liking my body, I wanted to be able to think nothing soon.

After the class, Portia stopped us and said, "Thank you, girls, for giving it a try. I hope I'll see you again."

She walked away and we giggled. "Oh my God, that was so hard," I said. "I am never making fun of my mom about yoga again."

"I know, right?" Shakina answered. "I thought this would just be stretching, but it was tough. Are you gonna come back?"

I wasn't sure whether to answer truthfully, but Shakina seemed nice enough not to mock me if I revealed that I was kind of into yoga. "Well, I have this problem with my heels, and my legs haven't felt this good since I was like eleven, so yeah, I think I'm gonna have to come back."

"Oh good. I didn't want to be the only one here. I have these back problems"—she gestured at her enormous breasts, which made me think maybe the pointy nubs had their advantages after all—"and I'm like you. My back feels like jelly right now. It's amazing."

"Cool! Hey, do you want to get a slice of pizza or something before the Saturday class?"

She smiled. "Yeah. Sounds great!" It wasn't until Shakina's mom picked her up and we said goodbye that I remembered that I was supposed to be sneaking out to a kegger with Lena on Saturday. Well, probably those didn't start at seven o'clock anyway, so I'd probably be able to do both. Still, I would much rather have gone to yoga class and rented a movie. But if my friendship with Lena wasn't exactly hanging by a thread, it was definitely changing. Me failing to be her wingman, wingperson, or person of wingness seemed like it might be a blow that our new, not necessarily improved friendship might not recover from.

I was thinking about this when Mom picked me up. "So how was class?" she asked brightly.

"It was okay," I said, and I was annoyed by Mom's big grin, so I didn't say anything else all the way home.

4

We won our game on Friday, 3–1. Of course I'm never happy with anything but a shutout, but it was still a respectable game. This time most of varsity was there for the second half. It was an away game and even though their bus was later than ours, they still got there forty-five minutes before their game, so what else were they going to do but watch us play? Well, sit in the stands and gossip and ignore our game, actually. Except for Lena, who watched and cheered. It made me happy to hear her voice.

Lena and I hadn't eaten lunch together again, but that was okay because I enjoyed hanging out with Shakina and Marcia.

Lena had called me Thursday night, and when we were on the phone, it was like we were our old selves again. Except, of course, that she never mentioned Conrad, and we were now dissecting every word and glance that came from a boy who might actually like her, and who she was probably going to kiss on Saturday night.

Here was a funny thing, though. Later, Conrad said to me, "Hey, you and Lena in a fight or something? She's never here anymore." Ack. I recognize a faux-casual question when I hear one.

"You are not allowed to go out with her. I want to be clear about that. And anyway she likes Duncan now."

Conrad got angry and defensive. "I was just making conversation! God, you are a pain in the ass sometimes!" He stormed off, proving that he did in fact like her. I know this made me evil, but here was an upside of Lena's new popularity: she'd upgraded her crush, which meant she and Conrad would not make my life horribly uncomfortable by acting on their crushes on each other.

So Lena and I were talking regularly, I was feeling more flexible, I liked my soccer coach, and everything was going great. Everything except Saturday night.

I suck at lying in general and to my parents in particular, and if I was going to lie to my parents and risk getting caught, I at least wanted it to be because I had a chance to make out with somebody instead of just helping somebody else make out.

I was a nervous wreck. And this was hard because Lena was so chipper and excited the whole time. The plan was that we were going to try the oldest trick in the book—the I'm-going-to-her-house, she's-going-to-my-house switcheroo—and then we'd each go back to our own houses after the party and tell our parents that we'd had a fight and didn't want to talk about it.

I guess it's such an old plan because it usually works.

Maybe. In any case, the first part went smoothly—I told my parents I was sleeping at Lena's on Saturday night, and they said okay without questioning or calling Lena's mom or anything. Why would they?

So far, so good. On Saturday I packed this enormous gym bag with my party clothes, my yoga clothes, and my yoga mat. I wore my hanging-out-with-Shakina clothes because I didn't want to be sitting around Demarco's, where there are frequently cute boys, in my tight stretchy yoga clothes.

Shakina was already at Demarco's when I got there. We got pizza and talked about the normal stuff for a while—who was cute, where we got our shoes, and, of course, soccer. I guess we were avoiding the topic of yoga because we were both still a little embarrassed about it.

"Well," I said, glancing at the time on my phone, "maybe we should head over and change and stuff."

Shakina nodded, then said, "Hey, thanks."

"For what?"

"Just for being the other new kid in yoga class with me."

"Oh! Well, it's not like I'm doing you a favor or something. I'm way more excited about yoga class than what's happening afterward. I have to go to some heinous party so Lena can make out with some boy."

"Can't she do that on her own?"

"Well, you know how it is. I guess I'm supposed to . . . I have no idea what I'm supposed to do, actually. I just know I don't want to do it. But I'm a horrible friend if I don't do it."

"Or else she's a horrible friend for making you do something you don't want to do."

Hmm. I hadn't really thought about that possibility. I tucked that away because I didn't really like the way thinking about it made me feel. It also kind of bugged me to hear somebody else telling me about my best friend.

"Anyway," Shakina continued, "should we go get our stretch on?"

"And our sweat. Don't forget the sweat."

"How could I? The other night when I came home was officially the first night my mom made me do my own laundry."

"Oh my God, really?"

"No, not really. It would have been, though, if my dad hadn't intervened. He was like, 'You can't punish her for doing something to help herself!' and my mom was like, 'You want to smell this bag?' "

We laughed. "So did he?"

"Oh no. The man loves me, but he's not crazy."

We walked over to the yoga studio, and when we got there, Rosalind was working the desk. She greeted us with "Namaste, bitches!" and we got a good laugh out of that. This time the class was a little easier despite the pizza sitting like a rock in my stomach, and even though I was really stressed about the party, I was, once again, able to forget the stress and everything else about an hour into the class and just be a sweaty contorted body that was breathing.

As I showered and changed into my party clothes, I couldn't help thinking that this had been a perfect Saturday night. I wished I could go with Shakina and get some ice cream or maybe just go home and watch a cheesy horror movie with my dad or read a book. Yeah, I'm a nerd.

And yet there I was getting my nerdy self into an outfit I thought would look good without looking like I cared whether I looked good and putting on makeup and all this junk, and I felt ridiculous. I walked out of the studio, and Rosalind was still at the desk.

"Big date?" she asked, looking at me in my clown makeup and ridiculous, ill-fitting clothes.

I shook my head. "I have to go to some party because my friend wants to go. I'd rather go home."

Rosalind smiled. "See, that's why I have Kim make me work on Saturday nights. It gets me out of a lot of crap I don't want to do."

"Yeah, well, maybe I should go put in some job applications."

"I'm telling you, it's a great strategy—you always have somebody else to blame. I have friends who think Kim is like some stepmother from a fairy tale when she's really like the nicest person on earth. I just blame her for making me work whenever I don't want to go out, which is usually."

"I'm definitely going to give it some thought," I said.

In fact, it was all I could think about as I got on the trolley and rode four stops to where I was meeting Lena. The whole way I was trying to sink into the seat because I was convinced somebody was going to see me and call my folks immediately and say, "She's not at Lena's!"

But nobody on the trolley seemed to pay much attention to me, and I hoped that we were whizzing past the people on the street too fast for anyone to know for sure it was me. Even though Charlesborough is right next to Boston, it can be a really small town sometimes, and you just never know who is going to see you and say something.

When I got off the trolley, Lena was standing there wearing a spaghetti strap tank top and what I would have said were her little sister's jeans if she had a little sister.

"How did you get out of the house looking like that?" I asked.

"I didn't," she said. She opened her purse and showed me the perfectly normal shirt she'd worn over the tank top when she left the house.

I felt kind of nauseous, and not just because Lena looked fantastic and I looked like a dork trying to look good, but also because I was still carrying a gym bag. I must have thought my other clothes would vaporize or something.

The whole thing made me uncomfortable, and yes, okay, I was jealous.

When we got to the party, it was clear that Lena was as nervous as I was. The music was loud, and there was a gross, sour smell in the air. As we wandered around, I felt weird and out of place. Still, it was kind of exciting. So this was a big high school party, the kind of thing that everybody there had probably lied to their parents about going to. I might feel weird and out of place, but it did feel like I'd joined the Real Teenager Club in some way.

In every room there were little knots of people standing around talking with beers in their hands. Some people were tapping their feet and stuff, but nobody was actually dancing. Not that Lena and I would have danced even if other people were dancing, but still.

It wasn't exactly like parties in the movies. In the movies, every room is packed with people, and the actors only know the other five actors who are starring in the movie. Here, there was lots of space to walk, and I recognized almost everybody from school. It was strange to see kids I saw in study hall with their heads buried in books laughing hysterically and spilling beer out of red plastic cups.

When we got to the back porch where the keg was, we finally saw somebody we knew well enough to talk to. Sort of. Courtney was holding a beer in her hand and looking kind of heavy-lidded.

"Hey," she said, "it's Lena and Alison!"

"Amanda," I corrected.

"Have a drink," she slurred as she poured beer into a cup.

I shook my head. "Designated driver."

Courtney stopped pouring and gave me a serious look. "That is so important. Oh my God, you are such a good friend. Designated driver. That is awesome. You are awesome. Hey!" she yelled over to a boy on the other side of the deck. "Jared! You got anything special for the designated drivers?"

Jared, whose party it was, yelled back, "Hell yeah!" He disappeared into the kitchen and came out a minute later with a paper plate holding a brownie with chocolate icing on it and handed it to me. "Here you go," he intoned. "You have sacrificed your own fun so that your friend can get home safely. You are a special friend, and you deserve a special treat."

"Uh, thanks," I said, taking the brownie. It wasn't like getting drunk was my idea of fun anyway, but I wasn't about to refuse chocolate.

"Zaleski!" Jared yelled. "You owe this fine young lady a sober ride home! You're designated driver next time!"

"You got it," Lena said, and we looked at each other and laughed. It apparently hadn't occurred to any of these people that we were still two years away from being able to drive.

"So what about you, Lena?" Courtney asked.

"Yeah, okay," Lena said, extending her hand to take the cup of beer from Courtney.

"Are you nuts?" I whisper-yelled at her. "You'll get suspended from the team!"

Lena frowned at me. "Manda, half the football team is here drinking. Look at Courtney. Do you think anybody takes that thing seriously?"

I couldn't argue with her because she was right. I mean, there was always the small chance that you could end up getting suspended from the team, but everybody said that only happened to people whose own parents ratted them out so they could get an extra punishment. I suppose I could have pointed out that she'd signed the thing, and even if nobody was going to hold her to it, her integrity was on the line, but that would have made me sound way more like Dad than I was comfortable with.

And I couldn't offer my real argument, at least not in front of other people: this isn't us, Lena. You have a built-in excuse not to dive into this scary thing, and you ought to take it. This isn't who we are. But I guess it was. Or, at least, it was who she was.

Pretty soon Lena was clutching my arm going, "Ohmy-GodohmyGodhe'shereohmyGodwhatamIgonnado?"

"Um, I don't know. Go talk to him?"

"Okay, but you have to come with me." So Lena and I walked over to where Duncan was standing with some other less cute, but still pretty cute, and tall, boy. If this was what second choice looked like, maybe it wouldn't be so bad having a popular best friend.

"Hey," Lena chirped at Duncan. It was all I could do not to roll my eyes.

"Zaleski," Duncan said. "'Sup."

"Not much. You remember my friend Amanda?"

"'Sup," he said. The whole opening-his-mouth thing was definitely detracting from Duncan's cuteness.

I looked at the other boy, and he looked at me. We both knew we were extra baggage here. "Hi," I offered in a tone I hoped was friendly, yet casual, and extended a hand to him, "I'm Amanda."

"'Sup," he said, shaking my hand. I guess he was in the Witness Protection Program or something because he didn't give me his name.

"Zaleski," Duncan said, "you wanna take a walk or something?"

"Yeah!" Lena practically screamed, and my eyes wanted very badly to roll, but I kept them in check, which is good because Lena shot me the "oh my God, I'm going to kiss him!" look.

I hoped the fakeness of my smile wasn't obvious as they disappeared into the backyard.

"So," I said to the Mystery Man I was left standing next to.

"Yeah," he said, and walked away. I wondered what kind of conversations he and Duncan had. Fascinating stuff.

In the movies, something earth-shattering always happens at parties. Something big breaks, or there's a fight, or the cops come. But this wasn't a movie, so I just sat there on the deck watching people come out back, get their beers, occasionally spill some on me and mutter an insincere apology, and leave. Nobody talked to me, and I didn't talk to anybody. I was incredibly bored, and I wished I'd thought to pack a book in my gym bag. I wound up looking at my heart rate monitor watch and seeing how low I could get my resting heart rate to go until finally I had been sitting there for half an hour by myself, and I thought, Well, this is officially the limit of what I'm willing to do tonight. I was tired and bored and I needed to be home. I grabbed my bag and walked into the backyard calling Lena's name. She didn't answer. I finally found her and Duncan with their arms around each other and their tongues down each other's throats. "Um, Lena?"

"Yeah?" she mumbled, untangling herself from Duncan.

"My dad's gonna freak if the Lexus isn't back by eleven," I said. Well, I figured if I was driving a fictional car, it might as well be a nice one.

"Okay," Lena said, and sighed. "Call me!" she squeaked at Duncan.

We walked back to the trolley, and Lena was talking and talking the whole time about how awesome Duncan was, but I was too annoyed to listen to her. And I was jealous. Even if Duncan himself was a little bit of a disappointment, I still wanted to be excited to sneak out and go to a party. I wanted to moon over some guy and have him want to kiss me. I wanted to be a high school girl instead of an overgrown kid.

"Call me tomorrow," she said as we got off the trolley.

"Will do," I answered.

"And, Manda?"

"Yeah?"

"Thank you. You are the best friend in the whole world."

I smiled in spite of myself. "Damn right I am."

I was hoping Mom, the more perceptive one, would be asleep when I got home, and Dad would be watching a movie. That way I could sneak my lying, beer-soaked self up to my room.

But of course Mom wasn't asleep. She was in her pajamas like three feet from the front door about to head up the stairs when I walked in. Perfect timing.

"Amanda! Is everything okay?" she asked.

"Lena and I had a fight," I said, and waited for her to answer, "That's not what her mom said, she's been worried sick," or something.

Instead she just said, "Really?"

This was why I wished it was only Dad I had to deal with. Because not only is Dad less perceptive than Mom, he is also completely transparent. If Dad had said, "Really?" like that, I would have known that he was actually curious about whether Lena and I had had a fight. But when Mom said it, I could just hear in her voice the possibility that she was going to call me on my lies, that this was my chance to either tell the truth and dig myself out of the hole a tiny bit or else lie some more and seal my doom.

"Yeah," I said, trying to put on a sad face.

And then I was sure Mom was on the level, which made this so much worse. She gave me a great big hug. "Sweetie," she said. "I'm so very sorry. You're really having a tough time of it these days. I'm sorry it's so hard. I wish there was something I could do to make it hurt less."

As much as I complain about being five feet ten inches tall, it turns out that feeling about one inch tall is even worse. Mom was showering me with sympathy and compassion I totally didn't deserve. I felt like I was looking at myself from the outside, this liar soaking up sympathy, and I suddenly remembered what I'd wanted to say to Lena: this isn't us. Well, this wasn't me. The whole lying-to-my-parents thing, the sneaking out to parties, the coming home drenched in beer and hoping that my parents had temporarily lost their senses of smell—none of it was me, and I was going to end it.

"Agh, Mom, stop." I pulled away. "Don't be nice to me. We didn't have a fight. We just snuck out to a party so Lena could meet some boy." Saying it out loud made me feel ashamed, but it was also a relief. I had gotten myself out of a lot of worrying about what would happen if they found out. Now I wouldn't have to lie anymore. I would probably end up grounded, but one way or the other I was going to suffer for tonight, so at least I was getting it over with.

"Dan," Mom called. "I need you."

"Okay, but the zombies are about to eat the biker's guts while he watches."

Mom gritted her teeth. "This is more important than *Dawn of the Dead*, honey."

Dad came out, saw me, and said, "What's wrong?"

"What's wrong," Mom said, "is that Amanda lied to us and went to a party tonight instead of going to Lena's house."

Dad's face suddenly hardened, and he said in this quiet voice that was so much scarier than if he'd been yelling, "Well. Let's talk about this."

So even though I was exhausted and needed to sleep, I had to go and sit in the living room while they asked me all kinds of questions. Whose party was it, who was there, had we been drinking, blah blah blah. Mom actually asked the questions; Dad just sat there and didn't speak. Dad never has nothing to say. I knew I was in serious trouble.

In the end, Mom told me I was grounded from anything but soccer and yoga for a month, and I had to give up my phone on the spot. Also I wasn't allowed to IM on the computer, which meant I could only use the computer with supervision, even though Mom always snoops on my computer use anyway.

I sat there and took it all without arguing. I felt like it was fair. Finally, Dad spoke up. "Amanda. I didn't think this was who you were. I'm really hurt, and I'm really disappointed." He left the room without saying anything else, and I felt hollow and despicable.

Fortunately for me, Mom gave me something to get mad about so I didn't have to focus all my energy on feeling guilty. "I'll call Rachel then," Mom said.

"What?" I nearly screamed. "You can't call Lena's mom! You can't!"

"Not only can I, I have to. She's my friend, Amanda. Did you really think I could keep this from her?"

"But now Lena's going to be mad at me for getting her in trouble! This is so not fair! I never would have told you if I had known you were going to get her in trouble too!"

"Just another example of not thinking things through tonight, I guess."

"But"—I was yelling now, and crying too—"she's going to hate me! You're going to kill our friendship!"

"She's not going to hate you," Mom said. "Maybe she'll be mad, but she won't hate you. It looks like she was going to get mad at you one way or the other. Maybe it would have been better if she got mad at you because you refused to go to the party."

"You don't understand anything!" I yelled. "I did the right thing! I told you! And you're punishing me for doing the right thing!"

Mom shook her head. "Amanda. Who ever told you doing the right thing was easy?"

5

I went to Lena's locker on Monday morning, but she was already walking away down the hall. There were a lot of people around, so I didn't want to yell or go running after her, especially if she was going to ignore me or be mean to me. I put a note in her locker: "I'm so sorry! Mom found out and I begged her not to call. I'm grounded from everything for the next month. U? Love, your best friend, Amanda."

I hoped that writing "best friend" there would make it still be true. But when I got to lunch, I was pretty sure that she saw me come in the door and turned away to talk to Duncan. I didn't think butting in on them would help my case any.

Besides, Shakina was sitting right there, and she smiled and waved and said, "Namaste, bitch!"

"Namaste, bitch!" I called back, and sat down with her.

"So how was the party?" Shakina asked.

"Nightmare. Total and complete nightmare. I sat there and watched boring people get drunk while Lena made out with a boy and then I got caught sneaking in"—I didn't want to admit that I'd been so wimpy about lying to my parents. God, I'd folded at the first sign of guilt. I was never going to be any good at being a teenager—"and I got grounded for like forever. I don't get my phone back for a *month*."

"Whoa. That sucks."

"Yeah, that's really the only bad part. I still get to go to soccer and yoga, and it's not like there are so many parties I'm dying to go to anyway. But yeah, it sucks."

"Did Lena at least apologize to you?"

"For what?"

"For getting you in trouble! Didn't you do this whole thing for her?"

"Yeah, but . . . but. No."

Shakina shook her head. "Well, I'm glad you get to go to yoga anyway," she said. "I was afraid you were gonna make me do the dead bug all by myself."

I was glad too. But not so glad that I could stop worrying about Lena and whether she was mad at me. I finally caught up to her in the locker room before practice.

"Hey," I said.

"Hey." Yep. She was mad.

"I'm sorry. You know I had no idea that I was going to get you in trouble, right?"

She whipped her head around and hissed at me. "No, Amanda, I don't know that. I don't know a lot of things. I thought you were my best friend, but you stabbed me in the back because you were jealous."

I stood there with my mouth hanging open for a minute before I could speak. "What? What are you talking about?"

"You're jealous of me and Duncan, you're jealous that I made varsity and you didn't, and so you deliberately got me in trouble to sabotage me!"

"I . . . how could you even think that? I would never do that! I just couldn't lie to my mom's face, and—"

"Oh, that was a great touch. Perfect little Amanda is *honest* with her parents, while bad Lena gets caught."

"You know, I got grounded too!"

"Like it matters. You don't have anywhere to go! How am I supposed to be Duncan's girlfriend if I can't even talk to him on the phone?"

She'd just thrown every one of my failures in my face, and she was gloating about Duncan, so I said something I probably shouldn't have: "Can the kid even put two coherent sentences together? What kind of phone conversations could you possibly have? 'Gee, Lena, I really like you!' 'Gee, Duncan, I really like me too! We're perfect together!'"

We had long since stopped being quiet, and when I looked around, I realized that a crowd had gathered to watch us yell at each other. I felt stupid, and mean, besides. I *had* been jealous of her. Was I trying to sabotage her chances with Duncan without even realizing it? I didn't think so. But I couldn't say for sure.

But Lena could.

"Bitch," she said, and turned away and kept dressing.

It's kind of funny how hearing that word from Shakina

just a couple of hours earlier had been funny, but now, spit out of Lena's mouth at me like that, it hurt worse than if she'd slapped me.

It was incredibly bizarre to be standing there in the locker room and thinking this was the moment that the best friendship I'd ever had ended. I really thought I had done the right thing when I told my mom the truth, but now I wasn't sure anymore. It didn't feel like there had ever been a right thing to do—just a bunch of wrong things.

I stood there stunned for a minute, then trotted out to the field, my eyes completely dry. Later, maybe much later, I would cry about this, but there was no way I was going to let Lena see how badly she'd hurt me.

I think every one of my teammates was probably thankful for Sever's disease that afternoon, because if I'd been able to run, I would have plowed through anybody who got in my way, and it might have been people instead of soccer balls that got pummeled. As it was, I had a shutout for the scrimmage. I wasn't letting so much as a mosquito get into my goal.

"Great intensity," Beasley said to me afterward. "Everything okay?"

And because I was tired and dripping sweat and I had grass stains on my legs from diving after balls, I answered, "Yeah, except for being grounded and losing my best friend, everything's just peachy keen."

Beasley did not do that annoying thing that a lot of adults do when they hear about kids' problems—that sort of frown that's really a smile that basically says isn't it cute that you have such silly problems. She didn't tell me I'd get over it or that it wasn't so bad. All she said was "I'm sorry. I know how hard that is."

"Yeah, well, I'll get through it. I'm tough as an old boot." I thought maybe saying it might make it true.

"I don't doubt it, Amanda," Beasley said. She gave me a kind smile and walked away.

I grabbed my stuff and headed home without showering, figuring I could be gross and smelly on the two-block walk home and shower there. That way I could avoid Lena and all the spectators who'd be hoping that Round 2 would start after practice.

Now that I was alone on the street, I started to cry. I just felt like my whole life had fallen apart. Everything I thought I was—good at soccer, Lena's best friend, a daughter who made her parents proud instead of crazy—all that was gone. I didn't know who I was anymore, and I missed my old self. I liked being that person.

I was so absorbed in my misery that I didn't hear the bike coming up behind me. I only heard Conrad's voice bellowing, "I just want you to know when you walk with the ball under your arm like that, it's really, really tempting to knock it out, but I know you're in a bad mood, so I'm not doing it."

I sniffled and turned to look at him. He was smiling, but I didn't feel like smiling. "Yeah, well, thanks for that," I said.

"No problem," he said. "I mean, I know going through school with that face all day can't be easy on you." He started to pedal away, but when he saw my unhappy expression, he got off his bike and walked next to me for a while without talking. It was nice, but annoying at the same time.

"So you should tell me next time you want to sneak out," Conrad said.

"Why?"

"Because I don't like the idea of you being at a party like that by yourself."

"Well, I was with Lena."

"Yeah, well, that's not much consolation. Jeez, I can't believe I used to like her." If only he'd told her, my life would be awkward because my best friend was dating my brother instead of because my best friend hated me. "Anyway," Conrad continued, "you really shouldn't go to parties like that without—"

"A chaperone?" I barked.

"Nah. Forget it," he said. I wanted to yell at him that I was fourteen years old and I didn't need him to protect me, but it was kind of sweet in a dumb, sexist way, and since Conrad was one of the few people in my life who wasn't pissed off at me, I decided to let it slide.

"I just mean," he said, "that I'm way better at lying to Mom and Dan than you are."

I couldn't help laughing. "Yeah, I guess it would be hard to be any worse than me."

When we got home I showered and did homework and ate dinner and did some more homework. Homework seemed even more boring than usual because I couldn't punctuate it with quick calls and messages to Lena. Even though I probably got it done faster, it still felt like it took forever.

Dad was giving me the deep freeze too, which also made

it weird to be in the house. It actually made being grounded a lot worse. Normally if Mom or Dad was being odd for some reason, I would have run to Lena's house. Now I had to sit there and feel the disappointment rolling off him.

At least my brothers were being cool. Whenever one of us is in trouble, we all pull together. So Conrad gave me an evening off from teasing, and Dominic gave me the evening off from annoyances. The three of us actually sat there and played a game of Crazy Eights that lasted for forty-five minutes and probably would have lasted longer if Dominic hadn't had to run off and watch some TV show.

So it was a slightly boring but conflict-free evening of sibling bonding, but I wasn't really surprised at the end of it when the switch in my brain that allows me to fall asleep didn't work again, and I just lay in bed thinking about how my heels hurt. I went downstairs and found Dad watching TV.

"Hey," I said.

"Hi," Dad said, not turning his gaze away from his show.

I sat down and watched for a minute. Some fishermen hauled a guy in a rubber monster suit on board and he killed them all. I don't know how it is that Dad can always find the crappiest horror movie on any channel at any given time. I guess it's a gift.

After a period of awkward silence, I finally said, "So, are you going to stay mad at me forever?"

And now Dad looked at me. "I'm not mad, Amanda. I am proud of you for telling the truth. I'm just kind of . . . Mom says I'm being stupid, but I thought maybe the fact that you and I had been through such a horrible time together would mean we wouldn't have to do the whole adolescent war of attrition thing."

"Dad, it's not . . . I shouldn't have lied, but—"

"Did it occur to you to ask?"

"What? No! I mean, you would have said no, right?"

"I know you well enough to know as soon as you signed that paper you wouldn't take a drink. So going to a party when I know you're not going to drink or get into a car with someone who's drinking and you have your phone with you? I probably would have gone for it."

Dad was nuts. There was no way he would have said yes to that. "And then Mom would have had to call Rachel, and we wouldn't have been able to go, and Lena would have been mad at me," I objected.

Now Dad looked at me like I was nuts. "But isn't she mad at you anyway?"

I watched as a humanoid from the deep claimed another victim on the TV. "You make a strong point, Father."

"That's why they pay me the big bucks around here," he said, smiling.

We watched the movie in silence for a while, but this silence was comfortable instead of awkward. "Do you ever sleep?" I asked.

"Not as much as I'd like. Lots to worry about, you know. I have to make sure I get all my worrying time in, and I'm so busy during the day that I need to carve out a few hours at night."

"What are you worried about?"

"You. Conrad. Dominic. That's mostly it right now, though of course there's always financial stuff too."

"Well," I said, getting off the couch—the crappiness of the movie had suddenly made me exhausted—"you don't have to worry about me. I'm tough as an old boot, remember?"

"I know you are. I love you, sweetie."

"I love you too, Daddy," I said. I climbed the stairs to my room and got probably the best five hours of sleep I'd had in a week.

6

The rest of the month was weird, but not because I was grounded. It was weird because it was the first month in six years when Lena wasn't my best friend. She seemed to be best friends with Courtney now, and Duncan was always all over her, so I guess he was willing to wait until she got her phone back. Since this was the main reason she had been mad at me, you'd think she might've cut me some slack. But you'd be wrong about that. She wouldn't say hi to me or even acknowledge my existence in any way. Which really didn't make her any different from any of the other girls on varsity or actually about 99 percent of the CHS student body, but still. In spite of everything, I expected better from her.

The worst part was that for the first two weeks there was this gigantic Lena-shaped hole in my life. At least eight times a day something would happen that I thought I couldn't wait to tell her, or I'd find myself bored in class and I'd get as far as turning to a blank page in my notebook to write her a note before I realized she wouldn't be reading any notes from me.

But then, as the days went by, the hole got smaller. It was definitely still there, but it shrank. I started to get used to having a life that didn't include Lena.

Kind of. In English class we started reading *Romeo and Juliet*, and we watched the movie and everybody got all gooey about how cool and romantic the whole thing was, and it seemed like Angus and I were the only ones in the whole class who weren't impressed. Also, I finally understood why Dad was pissed about being Friar Lawrence while everybody else got the studly fighting roles.

One day, after like the eighth girl had gone on about the beauty of tragic love, Angus finally spoke up. It was the first time he'd said anything in class outside of a small group, and everybody stared at him as he talked.

"You know," he said, his voice kind of shaking with anger, which was weird, but okay, whatever, "the tragedy here is just that these two are idiots. Romeo doesn't have any idea what love is. He thought he was so in love with Rosaline until he sees some pretty girl at a party, and suddenly he neglects his best friend so he can be with a girl he talked to for five minutes. His selfishness and stupidity get Mercutio killed. Mercutio is literally willing to die for Romeo, and all Romeo can think about is some girl he just met. And then they kill themselves because they're too stupid and selfish to think about any of the people they're leaving behind."

"Well," Mr. Gordon said, "that's certainly a strong opinion. What does everybody else think?"

Everybody else obviously thought the kid was a freak, but

I was glad that for the first time somebody had put their finger on what bugged me about the play—that everybody feels bad for Romeo, when it's really a tragedy for his neglected best friend. I said, maybe a little too loud, "I agree."

A couple of days later, I was walking toward the locker room when he came out of nowhere. "I wanted to say thanks," he said.

I just looked at him. "Um. For what?"

"For havin' my back in English class. You know? *Romeo and Juliet?*"

I stopped myself short of giving a laugh of surprise that might have hurt his feelings. The kid was thanking me for two words I said in class days ago! "Oh. No problem. I mean, you were right."

"Well, still, it was a nice thing you did. It was my brother," he added.

"What was?"

"The dying young thing. He killed himself."

"Oh my God. I'm so sorry. That's horrible."

"I found him."

"Oh God." What do you say to that? Nothing else but what I already said. "That's awful."

"Yeah. I thought I owed you an explanation. Since you told me about your mom. Anyway, I gotta go. I just wanted to thank you."

"Any time," I said. "I guess we're kind of in the same club."

It took him a second to figure out what I meant. "Yeah," he said. "Wish it was a better club." And then he walked away.

I half expected this to mean he would start popping up in the hallways and talking about death with me, but he didn't. I saw him in class, and sometimes in the halls, but we'd just wave, and it never came up again.

We had ten soccer games that month, usually with zero members of varsity cheering us on. We went 7 and 3, which was, as Beasley kept telling us, an awesome record that anybody could be proud of. (I allowed an average of 1.25 goals per game, not that anybody kept track of that.)

And I guess we would have felt better about our record if varsity hadn't gone 9–1 over the same stretch. They were a completely awesome soccer-playing machine. Geezer was still screaming at them all the time, and they never looked like they were having much fun, but they really could play. Lena was phenomenal, more than making up for Stephanie LoPresto's deficits in goal. She had two hat tricks in that month. I'm not going to lie—it was pretty impossible for me to cheer for her. It's not like I wanted anything bad to happen to her; it's just that every time I tried to yell some encouragement, it stuck in my throat. Luckily, everybody on my team was taking notes on the games so they could have a hope of starting in the next one, so whenever Lena did something spectacular, I wrote in my notebook so it would look like I was just a really intent student of the game instead of an ex–best friend with a chip on her shoulder.

I took a lot of notes.

In week three of my grounding, I went to the more forgiving of my jailers and asked if I might be allowed to grab a slice of pizza with Shakina. Dad said he thought that would be okay, and then he and Mom had a little fight about how he obviously didn't understand what being grounded meant.

But that's how I got to meet Shakina for pizza. It was such a relief to actually be able to talk to somebody I wasn't related to outside of school, especially somebody who wasn't mad at me.

It was hard not to compare Shakina with Lena. Shakina and I didn't have any kind of history together, so I couldn't just say "Mouse in the closet!" and have her remember how that happened in fourth grade. But on the other hand, we seemed to have more in common now than Lena and I did. We both thought all the boys in our class were doofs, we didn't want to go to parties and get drunk, and we would have been happy to stay up late watching stupid movies instead of plotting ways to sneak out and do stuff that wasn't really that fun anyway. The only problem was that I couldn't talk to her about Lena, because she'd just say what she thought, which was that she couldn't have been such a great friend to begin with if she'd dropped me so quick. This pissed me off because Shakina didn't know anything about the years Lena and I had together. But I guess it mostly pissed me off because I was afraid she was right.

Yoga was getting better and better. My heels definitely hurt less after soccer than they had in years, and if I still felt a little goofy doing some of the poses, at least I didn't feel goofy because I couldn't do it right anymore. I watched Portia, and I tried to be like her—tall, limber, confident, and beautiful— when I was walking around, especially before and after class.

I must have been getting pretty good at it, because when I strode out of the bathroom at Demarco's with my breath connecting my body and spirit or whatever exactly it was supposed to do, Shakina yelled out, "Portia! Namaste!"

Then I cracked up and went back to being myself, all knees and elbows instead of one gloriously harmonious body of interconnected parts. Still, it was nice to know I could make the attempt. As we ate our pizza, Shakina said, "It looks like varsity is going to states."

"Yeah. It definitely looks that way. Well, good for them. I'm not sure it would be worth it playing for Geezer."

"Right? She is too scary. Anyway, maybe she'll retire or die or something and then Beasley can coach us on varsity next year."

"That would be awesome," I said, and Shakina snorted. "Well, I mean, not the lady *dying*, of course." She kept laughing, and I knew I was never going to talk my way out of the horrible thing I had unintentionally said, so I added, "I mean, her dying would be cool, but I wouldn't call it *awesome*."

Shakina answered, "Not unless she took a soccer ball to the face and it broke her nose and drove it into her brain and she died that way. *That* would be awesome."

"You have given this way, way too much thought," I gasped out between laughs.

I guess it was pretty sick, the two of us cracking up about some old lady kicking the bucket and practically choking on our pizza, but it was the most fun I'd had in a long time.

In the car on the way home, I said to Mom, "You know, Shakina's family is new in town. I was thinking it might be nice to have them over for dinner. You know, to kind of welcome them to the neighborhood."

Mom gave me that "you're full of it" look. "You really have trouble with the concept of grounded, don't you? I guess you get that from your father."

"No! What? I mean, I wouldn't be leaving the house, right? What is this, solitary confinement, where I'm not allowed to receive visitors?"

"No, Amanda, it's a punishment."

"Mom. I lost my best friend. Don't you think that might be punishment enough?"

Mom didn't say anything for a while, and I hoped I hadn't overplayed my hand. I hoped she felt guilty about how Lena wasn't talking to me, since it totally wouldn't have happened if she hadn't called Rachel and squealed on us. On the other hand, I knew if she thought I was questioning whether she'd done the right thing, she would get stubborn and make sure I served every second of my sentence.

Finally she said, "Okay. If you give me their number, I'll call and invite them. So you don't have to go behind my back and ask your dad, which I know would be your next step." I looked over at her and saw she was smiling, so I dared to make a joke.

"Mom! I'm shocked you would even suggest that!"

She snorted.

7

We had a game the following Friday, and Shakina's family was coming over afterward. It happened to be the last night of my sentence anyway, so I guess Mom felt like she wasn't letting me out of too much punishment.

And, in fact, I had forgotten that hanging around Mom when she's preparing to have people over is a kind of punishment. She goes into freak-out mode and cleans frantically and yells at us for doing the stuff we always do, like not cleaning out our cereal bowls after breakfast. Dad always manages to disappear when this is going on. He volunteers to go buy napkins or whatever, leaving the rest of us to participate in the hurricane of cleaning. I guess this is probably because he'd get it worse than any of us if he stayed home, since he's the biggest slob of all.

So Thursday night while Mom was whirling around the house, Dad found some errand that he suddenly had to do, and that weasel Conrad volunteered to help him, like Dad can't carry napkins by himself. I got put on cobweb duty, which is really not that bad—I got to walk around with a dust mop and poke at all the corners—and Dominic was dusting.

"How come *she* gets to do the cobwebs?" Dominic whined. "I *never* get to do the cobwebs."

"You're not tall enough," I told him, and he stuck his tongue out at me.

The phone rang, and Mom called out "I'll get it!" mostly to stop Dominic from answering it, since after nearly a month of groundation, I had gotten used to the fact that the phone was a forbidden object to me.

"Oh, hi, Rachel," Mom said, and disappeared into the kitchen. The kitchen where, it occurred to me, there were probably a lot of cobwebs that needed removing. I poked my way into the kitchen, but Mom retreated into the dining room, and all I got to hear was "Mmmm." I mean, what does "mmmm" mean? It could be anything.

As it turned out, the kitchen was relatively free of cobwebs, but the dining room, well, now that probably needed some attention. It really did—every corner had a cobweb, and there were a couple of strands of web running to the light over the table, so I removed those. When Mom went to the bathroom, I couldn't pretend I had any cobwebs to remove, at least not while she was in there.

So I gave the hallway pretty thorough attention but couldn't catch any of Mom's conversation filtering through the closed bathroom door. Why is it that I can hear Dominic, who needs to eat some fiber, grunting every time he's in there even if I'm two rooms away, but I couldn't hear anything Mom was saying?

Finally I gave up, finished the cobwebs on the rest of the first floor, and then sat down to watch some TV.

Mom appeared about five minutes later and looked at me with my feet up. I could already hear the speech about how this is your friend coming over and you have to clean up your mess, blah blah, so I said, "Mom, look, the first floor is spotless!" Mom looked around trying to prove me wrong, and when she couldn't, she flopped down on the couch next to me.

"Well, thank God." She sighed. "Now we just have to keep your father and brother out of here until tomorrow night."

"Out of this room?"

"No. Out of the house. The minute they come in, they start spewing shoes and dirty tissues and change and empty drink bottles. Do you think I could call them and tell them to get a motel room tonight?"

"Yeah!"

"I don't think it would work. Just help me yell at them, will you?"

"If I have to," I said, smiling. "So, uh, how was your conversation with Rachel?"

"You mean you didn't manage to overhear the whole thing? It couldn't have been for lack of trying."

"Oh my God! I was clearing out cobwebs like you asked me to!"

She gave me this "who do you think you're kidding" grin, and then said, "Well, it was awkward. I'm a little frustrated with Rachel right now, to be honest."

"Why?" It was comforting to know that somebody besides me was frustrated with the Zaleski family.

"She called to ask if we wanted to get together tomorrow to celebrate the end of your grounding, and I had to tell her that you and Lena aren't really speaking right now."

"She didn't know that? Isn't that kind of weird?"

Mom looked slightly embarrassed. "I think so. But apparently Lena's been able to use her phone and computer for the last two weeks, and Rachel assumed it was you she was talking to all that time."

I exploded. "Two weeks! Two weeks she's had her phone back! The whole thing was her idea! That is so totally unfair!"

Mom gritted her teeth. "Well, Rachel and I discussed what we thought an appropriate punishment was at the time, but apparently she had a change of heart."

Could life get any more unfair? Lena got me in trouble and I ended up suffering more than she did. I hardly knew what to say.

"So Rachel wanted to know if you had any ideas about who Lena might have been communicating with for the last two weeks."

"Yeah, I've got some ideas, and so would she if she talked to her daughter once in a while."

Mom smiled. "Yeah, that's pretty much what I told her. Lena's grades are slipping, and Rachel's really worried."

I rolled my eyes. Like I cared about Mrs. Zaleski's worries.

I still couldn't believe Lena had been off grounding for two weeks.

"Listen," Mom said. "I know this is a really hard time, but let's just focus on the fact that we're having your new friend over tomorrow. There are a lot of good things happening too."

Well, I was glad that Shakina and her family were coming over, but losing Lena still hurt.

The next day after school, I was thinking so much about getting to practice to talk to Shakina that I forgot about trying to avoid Lena. So I walked into the locker room and there she was, right in front of me. She acted like I wasn't even there, and for some reason it made me furious.

"Are you ever going to get sick of pretending I don't exist?"

She opened her locker and pretended I didn't exist.

"I mean, you got ungrounded two weeks ago and I'm still grounded! How long are you going to hold this against me?"

Lena pulled on her uniform shirt. I really wanted to punch her just so she would have to admit I existed.

"Six years, Lena. Six years. I can't believe six years means less to you than a very stupid boy. You know what, on second thought, just keep pretending I don't exist, because I don't know you at all. I guess I never did."

She closed her locker slowly and walked out to practice with varsity and not watch our game. I threw my uniform on and slammed my locker door. I don't know how long I had been slamming my clothes and locker around before I realized Shakina was standing there.

"Well," she said, "I'm glad I'm not trying to shoot on you today."

This got a smile out of me, and I greeted my yoga buddy with "Namaste. I'm a being of pure light, breath, and energy."

"Yeah. I can tell. You wanna talk about it?"

"You know, I'm bored with the whole thing and it's happening to me. Tell me something that's happening with you."

Shakina talked about how her brother was annoying and how he got away with everything and she was supposed to take it because she was older, and she was ready to kill him. "He's so embarrassing. I'm sorry we have to bring him tonight. Mom said she wouldn't leave him locked up in his cage."

"All the boys can disappear and be annoying together, and hopefully we'll have a good time."

We won our game 4–2, which of course was a disappointing score to me, but I was happy because Shakina scored two of our four goals. I made two great saves near the end of the game to preserve the lead, and a weird thing happened— I heard an extra voice cheering me on. My parents and Dominic were in the stands sitting with Shakina's mom and a kid I assumed was her brother, and there were a few other parents in the stands, but somebody yelled out "Great save!" who didn't seem to be any of the usual suspects. And yes, attendance at our games is so pathetic that it's not just possible but actually quite easy to pick out the voice of every single person cheering for us.

I looked down to the end of the stands, and there, sitting by himself, was Angus. I didn't really know what to make of that, so I basically forgot about it. Or I tried to forget about it, but once we got into the locker room the rest of the girls wouldn't really let me.

"Hey, Amanda, who's your boyfriend?" Marcia asked.

"What are you talking about?" I said, even though I knew exactly what she was talking about.

"I mean, I didn't hear him cheering for anybody else," she said.

"Yeah, well, who knows. I mean, the kid is in my English class, and that's about it. So I have no idea."

"Yeah, right," she said. After a few more jokes about my cheering section from the other members of the team, the subject was dropped, and then when we went into the stands to cheer on varsity and take notes, he was gone. Varsity won their game and officially clinched their berth in the state tournament with two weeks left in the season. Lena was smiling and hugging Courtney and running around the field, and I had a lot of notes to take while everybody else was cheering.

I did not look at Stephanie, their goalie who allowed 2.43 goals per game to my 1.75, not that anybody kept track of such things, as she ran around celebrating.

I wondered for a minute: if I'd made varsity, would Lena have forgiven me by now? It's pretty hard to pretend somebody doesn't exist when you have to play on the same team. Or would we even have gotten into trouble in the first place? If I hadn't been so afraid of losing my connection to her, would I have said no to the whole stupid party thing? Or if I hadn't been so jealous of her, would I have felt like I had to tell Mom about it?

I guess you can drive yourself crazy thinking about what might have been, or how things might be different, but the fact is that you have to live in the real world where stuff can't un-happen. I wasn't on varsity, and Lena could never un-call me a bitch, and as much as I wanted to live in a world where she was still my best friend, that wasn't the world I was in.

I was pretty down about varsity making states because I am petty like that, so I had totally forgotten about Angus being in the stands for our game until Dad, on the car ride home, had to be corny and embarrassing and say, "So, Amanda, looks like you have a fan club."

Mom hit him on the arm.

"Dad, I barely know that kid. He's in my English class."

"Well, he certainly seemed to appreciate your play today," Dad said with this cheesy grin.

"Yeah, well, maybe his mom was late picking him up or something. I don't know."

"Really? Because, speaking as a man, I have to say that I never attended a girls' sporting event unless there was somebody on the team I had a special interest in cheering for."

Ugh, Dad was such a cheeseball. "Dad, I told you, I hardly know the kid, and, anyway, I'm like five inches taller than him! How completely ridiculous would that be?"

Dad suddenly lost his grin and got interested in the road, and I realized I'd just described his relationship with the woman who gave birth to me.

"Mom?" I asked, hoping for a lifeline from the woman who had hit her husband in my defense just a couple of minutes ago.

Mom turned around and looked at me. "Amanda, you dug this hole. You're gonna have to dig yourself out."

"Dad, you know what I mean. It's like I'm enough of a freak already, and—"

"I'll just say this and let it drop," Dad interrupted. "The average height of a man in this country is five nine. If you never look below that line, you are, by definition, going to miss out on half of the quality guys."

"Yeah, well, all other considerations aside, Dad, the kid's kind of weird and I do not like him like that."

"That's fine."

"I know it is! It's fine and it's none of your business. End of discussion!"

"I'm just—" Dad started, but thankfully Mom hit him again, and it really was the end of the discussion.

8

Dinner with the Williams family was great. Dad's special errand to avoid cleaning and Mom's wrath turned out to have been across town to the Asian market, and he made this four-course Asian meal that even I had to admit was delicious. The Williamses seemed to like it too: Shakina asked for seconds of the drunken noodles, which you don't do if you're just being polite.

And everybody seemed to get along really well. Both Dad and Mr. Williams love horror movies, so they spent the whole meal geeking out about which movies they'd seen, and their wives kept having to remind them that the dinner table wasn't really the greatest place to talk about severed heads.

Mom and Mrs. Williams talked about craft projects, and Shakina's brother, Jerry, worshipped Conrad as a god. As soon as dinner was over, all three boys went off to play video games and, like, fart and punch each other, or whatever dorky stuff boys do when they're together.

Shakina and I went up to my room and talked about how we couldn't find clothes that fit us. Whereas I could probably get away with an ace bandage, Shakina needed special sports bras that didn't even work all that well, and she apparently had trouble with tops like I had with pants.

"I don't know why they can't make clothes for real people," Shakina said. "I mean, who are these clothes made for anyway?"

Well, I reflected, not for the first time, they seemed to be made for Lena. But I didn't want to say that.

"I don't know. I mean, models are all tall, but pants don't ever fit me."

We were silent for a minute, and then Shakina asked, "So, you think we're going to have to go to every state tournament game, even if it's two hours away?"

"Is it even a question? You know what Beasley's going to say."

"Yeah, I do. I guess I just—this is wrong, but if I'm going to go halfway to Connecticut for a soccer game on a Tuesday night and fall behind in my homework, I'd rather be playing than watching."

"Yeah," I said. "Me too."

"Well, you actually could. I mean, you are better than their goalie. But, you know what?"

"What?"

"If you had made varsity we might not have gotten to know each other."

"That's true. And I would have had Geezer. And God knows what kind of trouble Lena would have gotten us into."

"It's weird. When we first moved here, I got like four e-mails a day from Emily—she was my best friend in Philadelphia—and then it went down to two, then one, and now I haven't heard from her in weeks."

"Wow. I'm sorry."

"Thanks. I don't get how we could be such good friends for so long and now it's like I don't even exist anymore."

"Yeah." I was getting sad and wanted to change the subject, so I suggested, "You wanna go down to the basement and throw the circuit breaker so the power goes out right in the middle of the boys' game?"

Shakina smiled. "That is evil! Of course I do!"

After the Williamses left, Conrad and Dominic went off to plot their revenge, and I was pretty sure I was going to regret my evil plan, even though it had been funny when we flicked the switch and the boys started screaming like somebody had killed them.

I found Dad in the kitchen washing dishes. "Hey, kid," he said. "Thanks for introducing us to such cool people. Raymond and I are taking Dominic and Jerry to the comic book convention next weekend!"

I stared at Dad. He'd actually used the words "cool people" and "comic book convention" in the same sentence. Well, as long as everybody was happy, I was okay.

"Yeah, they're nice."

"Go see Mom. She's got something for you."

I went into the living room, where Mom was watching some detective show. "Hey," I said. "Dad told me you had something for me."

"I do," she said, reaching into her purse. "Here." She pulled out a box with a new phone in it. A phone that played music and took pictures and was not Dad's five-year-old piece-of-junk hand-me-down phone that I'd been using.

"Oh my God! Really? I mean, is it really for me?"

She smiled. "Doing the right thing is never easy, but sometimes there are rewards."

Postseason

1

Varsity finished the regular season at 14–2. We ended up at 10–6, which would have been an amazing record if we weren't totally in the shadow of the magnificent varsity.

Our last game was at home, and Angus was there cheering for me again. It was weird, because when I saw him in English he didn't make any special effort to talk to me or anything. I mean, we were on the same side of pretty much every argument that started in class, but we didn't really talk directly to each other except to say hi in the halls.

Varsity was playing their first state tournament game at home. If they won that one, they'd play a regional game that would be within an hour's drive, and if they won that one, they'd play for the state championship somewhere halfway between Charlesborough and wherever the other team came from.

Beasley trained us well, because the entire junior varsity

showed up to the varsity's first postseason game with notebooks and pens even though our season was over and we couldn't earn starting positions for the next game. Maybe some girls were thinking about staying on Beasley's good side for next season, but honestly I did it without thinking—I just brought a notebook to varsity games the way I brought a notebook to history class. It was automatic.

So was varsity's victory. Lena didn't start, and she sat on the bench the whole first half. The game was tied 1–1 at the end of the first half, and Beasley turned to me and asked, "What did you notice?"

"That Geez—uh, Coach Keezer has a lot of confidence in Lena."

"What makes you say that?"

"I guess because she's got this whole strategy of turning the offense up a notch in the second half when the other team is tired, and she trusts Lena to be able to do that. Like, she could start her and then try to get a lead and hold it, but she doesn't. Even when they went down 1–0, Lena was still sitting there, but it's like her sitting on the bench is Coach Keezer's way of telling her that she knows she's going to score in the second half. It almost makes me feel bad for the other team because they'll be looking at a totally different offense in the second half."

Beasley smiled. "You want to coach JV next year, Amanda?"

I panicked. "You're not leaving, are you?" Somebody overheard this, and then the whole team peppered Beasley with questions.

Beasley motioned for us to lean in. "I wasn't supposed to tell you this. It's not public knowledge yet. Coach Keezer is retiring at the end of the year. So I'll be coaching varsity next season."

I suddenly got a lot more excited about next year. I could be playing for Beasley instead of having Geezer scream at me. I guess pretty much everybody thought the same thing because we all started saying, "Beasley, you have to pick me, you know I can play on varsity blah blah blah."

Beasley motioned for us to be quiet, but nobody would. Finally she pulled out her whistle and said, "Don't make me use this.

"Listen. Some of you will be playing on the varsity team next year and some of you won't. But remember that there are considerations about seniority that have nothing to do with playing ability, and, most important, remember that none of this has anything to do with what kind of people you are. Because you're all great people, and I've been really proud to be your coach."

Beasley's eyes were filling up as she said this, and Shakina yelled out, "Aw, Beez, we love you too!" I guess we probably would have had one big corny girly group hug if we could have done that in the bleachers.

The whole thing made me feel really good. Good enough that I felt like I could finally cheer for Lena. I remembered walking in on Dad and Conrad watching a baseball game once, and Dad was cheering for somebody on the Red Sox, and Conrad was like, "Dan, I thought you hated that guy!"

"That was when he played for the Yankees," Dad said. "He might be an asshole, but he's our asshole now."

I wasn't sure what word to apply to Lena, but whatever the right word was for her, she was ours.

Lena came streaking down the wing almost as soon as the half started, and she passed to Courtney while the stunned defenders were running at her. It was 2–1 before a minute had gone by in the second half. And I meant to cheer. I really did. Everybody else was cheering. It's just that when I opened my mouth, nothing came out. I ended up doing a lip-sync cheer while everybody else was yelling. The cheering turned to groans ten minutes later when the other team tied it up. (And just to prove that I'm a terrible person, not only was I not cheering for Lena in the biggest game of her life, but when Shakina leaned over to me after Stephanie let the goal in and said, "You totally would have had that," I whispered back, "Thanks!" because I knew it was true.)

When Lena scored the third goal, I was so caught up in the excitement of the game that I found myself cheering before I realized I was cheering for Lena for the first time in weeks. Varsity won, 3–2. Only two games from state champions.

"Okay," Beasley said after the game. "Next Tuesday in Worcester." Everybody groaned. Worcester was an hour away, which meant two hours of traveling on a Tuesday night. Our homework was going to be screwed up for the whole week. "The game starts at three, so you will be dismissed from school early to get on the bus." Everybody cheered. We turned to leave, and Beasley called out, "And, girls?" We stopped in our tracks and looked at her. "Leave the notebooks at home next time. We're just going to be cheering for our team."

2

The bus ride to Worcester turned out to be a ton of fun—we were laughing and singing the whole way. I would rather have been playing in the state tournament, but there was always next year with Beasley coaching. I could just imagine there wasn't a whole lot of laughing and singing on the varsity bus as they rode toward their game. They were probably sitting in stony silence while Geezer reminded them of every mistake they'd made in the last game.

The game was much closer than any of the other ones had been. Finally there was a team with an answer for Lena, which was their two *huge* defenders who probably could have started on our football team. They were slow, but the sight of those gigantic girls lumbering toward her definitely threw Lena off her game. When Charlesborough fell behind, everybody was probably thinking, Well, this was the same game they lost at the end of last season; at least the score was close this time. It's a season anybody could be proud of.

But Lena wasn't so off her game that she'd let the team down. I guess they got tired of chasing her or something, but Charlesborough was down 1–0 for most of the game, and then Lena and Courtney both scored within a minute of each other to put it away.

We were all hoarse from screaming, so the ride back home on the bus was a lot quieter. It was just starting to get dark, so nobody could really do homework, and everybody who cared knew they'd be up late trying to get everything done, so a lot of girls were napping.

Shakina and I sat in the back talking, mostly about how she thought this Rodney kid liked her because she was the only other black face he saw at school, but she kind of liked Jimmy Park, who was Korean and played basketball and was way too popular to notice her anyway.

When I lay in bed later that night, I told myself that I was not going to try to be Lena's friend or anything, but I would congratulate her if I saw her, the same way I would congratulate anybody on varsity. Maybe we'd never be best friends anymore, but we could at least be civil to each other.

The next morning, I saw Lena at her locker. I couldn't believe how horrible she looked. She was wearing pajamas, which a lot of teams did for spirit purposes, but usually when girls came to school in pajamas, they didn't look all crinkly and slept-in. Those girls did their hair and put makeup on and looked like they had slept. I know it's going to sound bitchy, but Lena looked like she'd slept in her locker and just crawled out. And that's saying something because she normally looks so good.

"Great game yesterday!" I said, as brightly as I could.

Lena raised her head, looked at me through bloodshot eyes, and said, "Thank you." I practically got drunk off her breath. I couldn't believe it! Lena was in school hungover, or possibly still drunk, looking like hell and reeking of booze. I mean, it was one thing to go to a party on Saturday night, but it was a totally different thing to show up at school on a Wednesday morning smelling like Saturday night.

I was so stunned that it took me a minute to realize that Lena had actually spoken two words to me for the first time in weeks. I wanted to ask her what the hell she was thinking, to tell her she needed to run home and get some mouthwash and probably fresh clothes or she'd get suspended from the team. But that was the kind of thing that a friend would tell you. And even though we'd just had a civil exchange of pleasantries, that didn't exactly make us friends again. I watched her shuffle down the hall and hoped for the best.

I went to the bathroom after second period, and someone also dressed in rumpled pajamas was puking. When Courtney emerged from the stall, she gave off the pleasant odor of booze mixed with puke. She looked, if it was possible, even worse than Lena had.

When I saw Stephanie in the hall, she had at least put makeup on and looked like she hadn't actually slept in the pajamas she was wearing, but she also smelled like she'd bathed in alcohol.

Right before lunch, the PA crackled and Ms. Allen, the principal, started talking. "Will the following students please report to the office." Ms. Allen proceeded to read the name of every single girl on varsity.

Everybody looked around. This was obviously bad, and it was huge. Entire sports teams did not get called out of class.

At lunch, JV sat together, buzzing and trading the parts of the story we knew. What we pieced together by the end of lunch was this: the entire varsity had spent the night at Kaitlyn's house to celebrate making the state championship game. One of the seniors had brought liquor, and they had basically been up all night drinking. Courtney was lucky to have puked in the bathroom, because Allison apparently puked right in the middle of her AP Bio class.

They were definitely getting suspended, but pretty much everybody thought Ms. Allen would let them back in school on Friday so they would be eligible to play in the championship game on Saturday.

"But they won't be able to play even if they do come to school on Friday," I said.

"What are you talking about?" Marcia asked.

"The alcohol pledge," I said. "It says you get a two-game suspension for your first violation."

"They'll make them sit out the first two games next season or something," Shakina said. "There is no way they won't let them play in the state championship game. There's just no way."

There was a way. By the end of the day, even though nobody had seen any of the varsity players since they were called to the office, the whole school knew: varsity had gotten a three-day suspension, and Ms. Allen was holding them to their alcohol pledge and suspending them from the next two games. They had drunk away their chance at the state championship.

I took a detour at the end of the day to check for Lena in the office. All I could see was an office full of parents, most of whom looked really angry. Lena's dad was right up in Ms. Allen's face yelling, "I'll have your job for this! I'm calling my lawyer!"

As I walked downstairs, I felt bad for Lena. Her dad had not been at a single one of her games, but if there was an opportunity to come in and scream at the principal, he was all over that.

At least Lena would get the chance to play for the state championship next year, with a coach who didn't yell and a goalie who could play. At least I hoped so. What about the senior girls? This was their last chance, and to know they'd come so close and ended their high school sports career by forfeiting the state championship game—well, I was glad it wasn't happening to me. I was annoyed with them for doing something so stupid, but mostly I felt bad for them. They had to be heartbroken and humiliated.

I couldn't wait to tell Dad because I knew he was going to go through the roof. He had been so outraged by the alcohol pledge, and even though we weren't friends anymore, my parents both liked Lena, and I just knew he'd be really mad.

But when I told him at dinner, he surprised me by saying, "Well, I guess that's what they get."

"But, Dad, it's totally unfair! Lena's dad is going to sue the school."

"Oh, Avi cares about his family all of a sudden?" Dad

said, and we looked at him like you do when somebody says something that everybody's been thinking but nobody has had the guts to say.

"Dan," Mom scolded, but you could tell from her tone of voice that her heart wasn't in it.

"Dad, you were the one who said the pledge was a sham document and . . . something else bad, I don't remember."

"I was objecting to it at the proper time," Dad said. "If people had refused to sign and were suing the school so they would be allowed to play anyway, I would be in total support of that. But they did sign it, Amanda. So they agreed that what they do outside of school is the school's business. They had no problem with the rule until it was enforced on them. Suddenly they think it's not fair. Where were they two months ago? It was fair enough before."

"But Lena's not going to get to play!"

"Well, I hate to say this, but she should have thought of that before she showed up drunk at school. She signed the document, Amanda. She knew what the consequences were. What baffles me is that they didn't even try to hide it. I mean, my God, in my day—"

"Dan, is this really a story you want your high-school-age children hearing?" Mom interrupted.

Dad thought for a minute, then spoke. "Maybe not. But the point is, when you don't even try to disguise your bad behavior, you're practically daring the authorities to punish you. Did the girls think they were so special that they wouldn't get in trouble for something anybody else would have gotten in trouble for?"

"But nobody else does get in trouble," I said. "It's like you said. Everybody knows the hockey and football players are out getting hammered every weekend."

"But do they come to school and flaunt the fact that they've flouted the rules?"

"Did you really just say 'flaunt the fact that they've flouted'?" Conrad asked.

"Yeah," Dad said. "It's perfectly good English. What's the problem?"

"I guess, no, you don't see the hockey team puking in their bio classes," I said, ignoring their linguistic debate.

"There you go. There's an unspoken agreement, which I think is incredibly dumb by the way. The school makes you sign this unconscionable invasive pledge, but they don't have the resources to police every house in town, so they ignore it until somebody makes it impossible for them to ignore it."

"But isn't that kind of—" I started.

"Corrupt? Dishonest?"

"Yeah."

"Absolutely. Which is why I'm going to address the school committee about it after the end of the school year," Dad said.

We all gasped. "Dan," Mom warned.

"Diane. How could this possibly humiliate anybody? No one knows what happens at school committee meetings. Quick, Conrad, what happened at the last school committee meeting?"

Conrad shrugged. "Something boring?"

"Sean Calendar's dad asked that any book containing, and I quote here, 'the F bomb' be removed from the high school library."

"Sean Calendar? The kid who sells weed in the parking lot?"

"I don't know about Sean's extracurriculars, but yes. Who's talking about this at school?"

"Nobody," I said.

"Exactly," Dad said. He looked pleased with himself. "Anyway, it's a dishonest, corrupt, and completely moronic pledge, but we signed it and, in so doing, signed on to the corruption it implies. I guess you can see why I'm not all that sympathetic to everybody crying about it now."

I could. But I still wasn't sure exactly how I felt. In a way, Dad was right, the varsity was almost daring the school to punish them—look at us, the perfect little girls' varsity soccer team, we don't get in trouble, that's for other kids. On the other hand, it did seem unfair. Like a really harsh punishment for what wasn't all that serious an offense. Except it kind of was.

I didn't know how to feel or what to think.

It only got worse the following morning. Right in the middle of homeroom, Ms. Allen came on the PA again, and this time it was the entire JV team she wanted to see.

The walk from my homeroom on the third floor down to the office seemed to take a year. I knew I hadn't done anything wrong, but I couldn't help being afraid. I never got called to the principal's office. And I couldn't even rehearse a lie to get out of whatever trouble I was in because I had no idea what I could possibly be in trouble for. Were we going to have to provide an alibi for the other night?

Our whole team crowded into the principal's office, along

with Geezer and Beasley. All the adults had very serious faces on, which is never a good sign.

"Girls," Ms. Allen said, "I know how fast news travels in this school, but I wanted you to get the full story from me. As you probably know, the girls' varsity soccer team had a party after their game on Tuesday night, and many of them came to school the next day showing obvious signs of having consumed alcohol. In accordance with the zero tolerance pledge, everyone who attended that party has been suspended from the next game, which, as you know, is the state championship. Coach Keezer?"

Geezer, dressed in sweats as she always was, said in her sandpapery, gruff voice, "Our opponent expects to play a soccer game on Saturday. Now, with the entire varsity ineligible to play, that leaves us with two options. One is to forfeit the game. The other one is to play the game with the only eligible interscholastic players we have." She looked at us like she'd just said something significant, but for some reason, maybe because it was early in the morning, I just wasn't getting what she was saying.

Beasley spoke up. "You are Charlesborough High School's only girls' soccer team right now. And we've agreed to leave this decision in your hands, but what we're asking here is if you want to play for the state championship on Saturday."

I don't know if all the air was sucked out of the room, or if it just felt that way because nobody was breathing.

"We're going to leave you alone and give you girls a few minutes to talk this over without us," Ms. Allen said, and she and Geezer and Beasley walked out of the office.

The door shut with a click, and we looked at each other. Well, no. That's not true. Actually everybody looked at me.

Marcia asked, "What do you think?"

"I . . . it feels weird, like we didn't earn it," I said, and I saw heads nodding. "I mean, I wanted to play in that game as a member of the team that got there."

"But if someone had gotten injured," Shakina said, "they would have called one of us up to take the roster spot. Would you have refused to play in the game if you were filling in for somebody who was hurt?"

"No. I guess I wouldn't. And how many state championship games are we going to get a chance to play in?"

"Three after this year," Denise called out, and everybody laughed.

"Maybe, probably, I hope so, but we don't know. I guess in the end, I don't see how we can say no. Is there anybody who feels like they can't play?"

"Varsity's going to hate us," Nina announced.

"Yeah," Shakina said, "but at least they'll finally know our names."

"I'm scared of playing for Geezer," Marcia whispered, and we looked at the door, like maybe Geezer was on the other side of it listening with a stethoscope or something.

"Me too," I said. "I'm scared of getting yelled at, I'm scared of playing a team so much better than us that we get humiliated, and I'm scared of the varsity girls hating us. More than they already do, in my case," which got a laugh from everybody. "But I guess the thing I'm most scared of is sitting on my bed on Saturday afternoon listening to my brothers being annoying and thinking, 'I could be playing for the state championship right now.' I don't know how you guys feel, but that's actually scarier to me than any of the other stuff."

I wasn't expecting everybody to cheer and carry me out of the office on their shoulders or anything, but I guess I wasn't expecting the dead silence that followed my little speech.

After what seemed like an hour, Marcia said, "So, uh, should we take a vote?"

"Okay," Shakina said. "All opposed to playing the game, raise your hands." Nobody raised their hand. "All in favor?" Everybody's hand went up, and suddenly we were cheering.

The door opened, and the adults came back in with big grins on their faces, even Geezer, which totally shocked me. "Okay, girls," Ms. Allen said. "I guess your decision is pretty clear, but can you keep it down so we can run a school out here?"

"Call your parents," Geezer said, "and tell them you have soccer practice today and tomorrow. I'll give you some time to get cleats and pads after school today, but be back here at three-thirty."

I floated out of the office and through the rest of my day. When the day finally ended, I ran home and got my soccer stuff and ran back. Nobody else was there yet, and my heels were killing me from running so much, so I lay on the ground in the goal and did a couple of yoga positions and tried to shut my brain up until Marcia finally showed up and agreed to shoot on me.

3

Marcia got at least twelve goals past me. I was nervous about the game, but mostly, for right now, I was nervous about playing for Geezer.

If you made a mistake for Beasley, she took you aside and asked, "So what happened on that play?" and you told her the mistake you'd made.

If, on the other hand, you made a mistake playing for Geezer, you got reamed out in front of everybody. I honestly didn't know how Stephanie managed to play so many games without crying. I wasn't sure I'd be able to do the same if a goal went through and Geezer started screaming at me.

Finally the whole team was there, and some more girls lined up to shoot on me, probably because they saw me sucking out loud at stopping Marcia's shots and they figured they'd never get a better chance to get one past me. A bunch of the other girls were running passing drills.

Finally we saw Geezer walking across the field with

Beasley trailing behind her. Geezer looked at her clipboard, and we all stopped in the middle of whatever drill we were doing.

"Take a knee, girls," Geezer barked, and everybody gathered around and went down on one knee, which was an incredibly uncomfortable position but apparently traditional. Beasley always just let us put our butts on the ground. One more thing that was going to be weird and different about playing for Geezer.

"I've seen you girls in the stands at every game, usually taking notes, so you probably know a lot about my coaching philosophy already." We nodded.

"So I don't have to tell you that I hold my players to a very high standard." Nobody gave even a ghost of a nod to this one. Geezer's voice sounded funny, and it could really only be a matter of time until she started to yell.

"I don't want you to think those high standards are only for the players. I have the same high standards for myself as well. What happened on Tuesday night was not just an error in judgment on the part of my players. It was a failure of leadership. I am the coach of that team, and it's clear to me now, as painful as it is to face, that my work with the varsity team has not been up to my standards. I coached a team that willfully disregarded the rules, a team that clearly has a great deal to learn about integrity and fair play."

Okay, she was pissed at varsity. Big surprise. But why was she telling us this when we had a game to practice for?

"I grew up in Texas, and in Texas we have a saying: you dance with them that brung you. Ms. Beasley, this is your

team, and you'll be coaching them through their two practices and the game on Saturday."

I felt like I was exhaling for the first time. We weren't
going to have Geezer screaming at us! At least that was one less
thing to worry about.

Beasley looked totally shocked. "But, Elaine," she said in
a quiet voice, "you can't do this. This is your last game!"

Geezer's voice actually broke when she spoke, which was
something I certainly never expected. "Carolyn," she said,
"My . . . my career is . . . I have thirty years of coaching under
my belt, and it's not defined by one game. My team ended
their season on Tuesday just as sure as if they'd lost the game.
This is your team, and it's your game."

Beasley had come within about a half second of saying
something bad about Geezer like eight times in the season, and
it was clear that she didn't think much of Geezer's coaching. So
this made it even weirder that they suddenly hugged, and Beasley had to wipe tears out of her eyes before she talked to us.

"All right, girls. We've got the biggest game you've ever
played and the biggest game I've ever coached on Saturday.
Let's get to work!"

When she said this, the cheer that had been building up
ever since Geezer said she wasn't coaching finally burst out.
We practiced until the lights came on at the field, and when
Beasley finally let us go, I knew I should have felt exhausted,
but I was so hyper I felt like I could play all night.

Which I guess was a good thing, because Shakina came
up to me in the locker room and said, "Are you going to yoga
tonight?"

"Hell yeah I'm going to yoga!" I bellowed. "I'm gonna show those bitches how a champion salutes the sun!"

"Whoa," Shakina said. "You been chugging those energy drinks again?"

"Ugh, no way. I just—" I wanted to say something about how I would not possibly be able to sleep until Saturday if I didn't get to clear my mind with some yoga, but I guess I was still a little embarrassed about how much I liked the meditation part, even with Shakina, so what I ended up saying was "It's helped my heels so much that I can't imagine not doing it before such a big game."

"Cool," Shakina said. "Because my back is hurting."

"I'll see you there, then!"

"Count on it," she said, and walked away.

I bounced home, where Conrad was sitting on the front porch reading. "Wait a minute!" I exclaimed. "Are you actually doing homework? What's the occasion?"

He smiled. "Yeah, I figured if your sorry butt is playing in the state championship, pretty much anything is possible."

I bounced my soccer ball off his head and compared him to a pretty nasty part of the human body. And then I realized why he was doing his homework. "You've got a crush on Ms. Cooney!" I yelled.

He obviously did, because he looked all around and said, "Shut up! That's totally not true."

"Oh yeah, you just started doing the reading on your own. It has nothing to do with her leaning those C-cups over your desk and telling you she thinks you can do so much better . . ." I was laughing, and Conrad threw his book at me and compared me to an even grosser anatomical part.

I was thrilled to have gotten the best of him, and then, as I opened the screen door, he said, "Amanda."

"Yeah?"

"Seriously, good luck on Saturday."

"Thanks!" I said.

Later, Mom dropped me at Charlesborough Yoga Studio. "You know, it's okay to skip this," she said. "I don't want you pushing yourself too hard."

"Mom, if I don't do something to calm myself down, I'm going to end up throwing Conrad down the steps just because I can."

"Well, if it will keep my delicate son safe, then I guess it's okay," Mom said, smiling.

I walked into the studio. Rosalind wasn't behind the desk, which was kind of a relief, because if she was there, I'd have to make small talk about the game, and all I wanted to do was not think about it for an hour and a half.

I didn't manage that, but for about twenty minutes in the middle of class, all I did was sweat and move and not think. It felt great.

4

Friday was a blur. I guess there were classes, and I'm pretty sure there was a long practice, but the whole time I was in goal in the state championship. It was hard to know that at some point in the state championship game, maybe a bunch of times, it would come down to me and some girl with the ball, and I wasn't going to be able to win every one of those. I had had only one shutout in the whole season, and that was playing other JV teams, not playing the best varsity players in the whole state.

I knew that we probably couldn't win this game, but I didn't want to be the one that made us lose. I couldn't stand the thought that on Monday at school, everybody else would get told they had a good game, even if they'd made a mistake that allowed the other team to get a shot on me. And if I let like six goals through, nobody would tell me I had a good game, at least not sincerely. I couldn't win the game for us, but I could lose it.

In a way, it felt like my entire high school career was on the line. If I played well, I'd be a hero, and if I didn't, I'd always be the girl that humiliated CHS, the girl who couldn't really play.

I lay down in my bed that night, but I didn't know who I thought I was kidding. I stared at the ceiling for a while. I closed my eyes and tried to breathe, tried to find the same kind of serenity I felt at yoga class. No luck. I guess the breathing wasn't enough—I had to be bending and sweating too.

I tried to think good thoughts about stopping every single shot on goal, but I knew that was just a fantasy, and my fantasy of a shutout kept turning into horrible visions of goals raining down on my head and bleachers full of people booing me. Or sometimes I pictured Beasley pulling me because I obviously couldn't play that day, and walking off the field and having the fans of the other team cheer wildly for everything I'd done for them.

Finally I got up and wandered downstairs.

I wasn't surprised to find Dad down there. What did surprise me was that he had a big movie theater tub of popcorn on the coffee table along with a box of Milk Duds and two gigantic sodas in movie theater cups.

"What took you so long?" he asked, smiling.

"Dad, where did you get this stuff?"

"You know that paper supply warehouse in Jamaica Plain?"

"Of course I don't! What the hell are you talking about?"

"Yeah, well, anyway, that's where I got the movie theater cups. I had to buy like fifty of these popcorn tubs, so we're going to have to make this an insomnia tradition for the next ten years or something. Check this out!" he said, turning the popcorn tub toward me. I saw red cursive writing there, but my eyes were still adjusting to the light. "Enjoy the show!" Dad chirped. "How cool is that!"

"So you made this whole insomnia plan, with the Milk Duds and everything?"

"Well, I thought I'd be prepared in case you weren't sleeping."

"Dad, you knew I wouldn't sleep. The biggest game of my life is tomorrow!"

"Right, and remember two things about that. The first is that whether you sleep or not is not going to affect you. You'll have the adrenaline to carry you through. So you don't have to stress about not sleeping."

"You know, I'm so stressed about everything else that I totally forgot to stress about that."

"Great!"

"Until now." Dad's face fell a little, and I had to add, "Just kidding."

"Okay. The other thing is, and I haven't said this because Mom tells me I'll annoy you, but she's asleep now, so here goes. This is a totally high-pressure situation for the other team, and completely low-pressure for you."

"How do you figure that?"

"Imagine you're on a varsity team. How's it going to look if you lose to the JV from another school? That's going to be a humiliating defeat. But for you guys—I mean, if you win the game, it's a spectacular, almost miraculous victory, and if you lose, well, you're playing a much better team than you've played all season. JV is supposed to lose to varsity. You know what I mean?"

"I guess." It seemed both parents were right. Mom was right that Dad was annoying, but Dad was also right that I hadn't really thought about the whole thing from the perspective of the other team, and when you looked at it that way, it seemed like we had everything to gain and nothing to lose. But for some reason it's always really hard for me to hold any reassuring thought like that in my brain for very long.

I sat down in the chair and asked, "So, what's our movie selection for tonight?"

"Jamie Lee Curtis double feature. The queen of scream in *Terror Train* and *Halloween*. What's your preference?"

"You actually rented movies?"

"Yeah. Like I said, I wanted to be prepared in case you couldn't sleep."

I looked at Dad for a second, and I immediately knew that he'd planned this not just for me, but for him too. Even if by some weird chance I had managed to fall asleep, there was no way Dad could sleep with me about to play in the state championship. It was really sweet, and it was even better because Dad didn't say anything about it and get all goopy.

"*Halloween*, I guess."

"Good choice. A classic that's widely believed to have created the entire slasher movie genre."

"What an achievement."

We watched, ate popcorn and Milk Duds, and sipped our

caffeine-free sodas. It was really pleasant, except that every time Dad reached for popcorn, he gestured to the writing on the side and asked, "Enjoying the show?"

Like the eighth time he did that, I finally said, "Dad, it's not that funny. It's actually not funny at all."

"Eh, I'm amusing myself," he said, and grabbed another handful of popcorn. "Real butter, you know. Can't get that at the movie theater. None of that 'topping' stuff here. Isn't it weird how they ask you that? 'Would you like topping?' What is that stuff, anyway?"

"I don't know, Dad. Hey, can I ask you something?"

"Of course. Unless it's about what's in movie theater topping."

"Agh, Dad, nobody but you even cares about that."

"Okay. So what is it?"

"Why did you—I mean, if you were planning this big insomnia party, why exactly did you pick these movies?" As soon as I said it, I realized I'd made a mistake, because Dad might admit to some teenage crush on Jamie Lee Curtis, which I didn't want to hear about, or worse yet, he'd find some way to start talking about Mom—the dead one—and he'd get weepy.

He surprised me, though. "Because," he said, "these movies, despite the knife-wielding maniacs, are fundamentally upbeat and positive."

"Dad, what could you possibly be talking about?"

"Look, here's a girl, a very tall girl, by the way, one who was a sex symbol to millions"—he was getting dangerously close to admitting a crush, but he swerved away at the last minute—"a girl who is beset by problems that would crush most people. That *do* crush, or more accurately slice and dice, most people. She's pulled out of her normal life and forced to be strong in order to survive. And she has the strength not just to endure, but to prevail. That's what these movies are fundamentally about, kid. They're about finding strength you didn't know you had. You know what I mean?"

"Honestly, Dad, I kind of tuned out about halfway through that speech."

Dad laughed and said, "Okay, I'll shut up. This is the best part anyway."

We watched as Jamie Lee Curtis shoved a coat hanger right into the masked killer's eye, and sometime later, I woke up covered in popcorn with Dominic watching *The Fairly OddParents* on the TV.

5

I sat bolt upright. "Oh my God! What time is it?" I yelled.

Dominic looked at me like I was incredibly dumb. "*Fairly OddParents* comes on at seven-thirty," he said. "And it's almost over, so I guess it's almost eight."

"I'm going to be late! Why didn't anybody wake me up?" I bellowed to the rest of the house.

Mom came running into the room. "Will you please stop yelling," she whispered. "Conrad's still asleep, and you know what he's like when he gets woken up this early."

"But my game!" I said.

"Amanda. Your game starts in five hours. I think you'll make it in plenty of time."

"But we're supposed to be at school two hours before the game so we can get the bus and get to the field—"

"Sweetie, school is two blocks from here. If you decided to crawl there, you'd still be two hours early. Now just relax. Come and have some breakfast."

"There's no way I can eat. I'm totally nauseous."

"Too bad," Mom said. "More brioche French toast for me."

Dominic and I followed her into the kitchen. She'd done that special occasion thing where she went to the bakery and got the sugar brioche loaf I loved—it was all eggy and sweet to begin with, and then she'd coat it in her vanilla French toast eggy goo and fry it up with almonds on the outside. It was too delicious for words. And Dominic was too much of a goofball to appreciate it.

"Ew," he said. "Not that gross stuff! I want Golden Grahams."

I looked at Mom, wondering if she was going to give him the smack upside the head he so richly deserved. Sadly, she didn't. She never did. "Why don't you go turn off the television, and then you can pour yourself a bowl of Golden Grahams," she said through a smile that was clenched a little too tightly to be real.

"Can't believe I have to pour my own cereal. Miss Special Soccer Star gets whatever she wants, but . . ." He kept talking, but he'd gone to the living room to sulk about how Mom wasn't waiting on his ungrateful self, so we couldn't hear him anymore.

"Okay, let's have some breakfast, shall we?" Mom said.

I was still feeling a little groggy, and I looked over at the stainless steel carafe of coffee that Dad had set up to brew on a timer. Dad was nowhere to be seen—maybe he'd stayed up for the second half of the double feature.

"You think I could have some of that?" I asked, gesturing at the coffeepot.

"Oh God, I knew this day would come. Your dad will be so proud of you." Dad was a total coffee fiend, and he was the only one in the house who could stand the stuff, so we all teased him about it.

Except that right now it smelled really good, and I thought it might help with the grogginess. "Do you want to wake him up and hear a lecture about the proper ratio of cream and sugar, or are you going to live dangerously and mix a cup up without instructions?" Mom asked.

"I guess I'll go for it," I said. I poured about two-thirds of a mug full of coffee, then topped it up with half-and-half and stirred in a packet of Splenda.

I took a tentative sip. It was sweet and creamy and bitter and awful. I started laughing. "Now I know why Dad likes this."

"Why?" Mom said. "It's still a mystery to me."

"Because it's like life," I said, smiling and taking another sip. Mom looked at me like I was nuts, but I knew when I told Dad he would totally get it.

Of course, Dad was going to be all over me to talk about my feelings, which was going to be incredibly annoying, whereas Mom just made me a delicious breakfast and ate it with me without asking anything about how I felt.

"Hey, we're invited to the Williamses' house after the game," Mom said. "I said that was fine. I hope it's okay."

"Yeah," I said. "Weird that Shakina didn't mention it to me."

"I don't think she knew. You know, sometimes we parents actually think and act independently of our children."

"Really? Why?"

Mom laughed. "Reminds us of our lost youth, I guess."

We ate the rest of our delicious breakfast, and sure enough, Dad showed up, and the first thing he asked was "So, how are you feeling today? Feeling good about the game?"

Mom swatted him. "If she wanted to talk about it, she'd be talking about it. Don't be annoying."

I mouthed "Thank you" to Mom, and then said, "Hey, Dad, guess what I had to drink this morning? Cup of coffee!"

Dad's face lit up like I'd just told him I won a Nobel Prize or something. "How'd you like it?" he asked.

"I like it. It's like life."

Sure enough, he smiled and nodded. "It certainly is, my dear," he said, "it certainly is."

"You're both nuts," Mom said. I cleaned up the dishes with Mom, and then, before Dad could annoy me by asking about my feelings again, I ran up to my room to call Shakina so I could talk about my feelings.

"I'm totally freaking out," I said.

"I know. Me too. I hardly slept at all."

"Me neither. But I'm strangely hyper. But maybe that has something to do with the coffee."

"Oh, great—caffeine again. I guess we can look forward to some screaming then," she said.

"Probably." And then, "It's gonna be okay, right?" I nearly whispered. "I mean, whatever happens, it's going to be okay."

"It's already okay," Shakina said. I took a minute to digest that.

"That's deep."

"Namaste, bitch."

"Namaste, bitch. See you later."

"Okay."

Mom knocked on my door. She had a yoga mat under her arm. "Hey, I'm going to hour of power over at the Charlesborough Yoga Studio. You wanna come, or do you have a full schedule of fretting and barking at your brothers?"

"Well, when you put it that way, okay."

So Mom and I went to hour of power, but it didn't help much. For one thing, it's usually only at the hour mark that I can turn my brain off, so I didn't get that nice sensation of not thinking. But even if it had been a ninety-minute class, I don't think I would have been able to do it. Not today.

We went home and I showered, which was probably stupid since I was going to go get all sweaty again, but whatever.

"You want a ride to the bus?" Dad said when I got downstairs. I struggled to remember that he was trying to be nice and not just treating me like a little kid who couldn't walk two blocks by herself, so I said, "No thanks. I think a little fresh air will be good for me."

"Okay," Dad said. "We'll see you there, sweetie. You're awesome." He gave me a big hug, and then Mom came over and gave me a big hug and Dominic gave me a big hug, and even Conrad, who had just gotten out of bed, shuffled over and punched me on the arm. "Kick some ass," he said.

"I'll do what I can."

6

The game was in some suburb about forty-five minutes away. As we rode the bus in silence, I remembered how much fun it had been to ride to watch the varsity regional game, and how I'd imagined how tense the varsity bus was. Well, we were varsity now, and even though Geezer was sitting quietly in her assistant coach role and not screaming at anybody, it was quiet and tense and no fun. I couldn't help feeling like we were being led to our doom. All I could think about was the air full of balls I couldn't stop, the humiliation I would feel when I got scored on in the state championship.

I hadn't told anybody this, but I felt like anything but a shutout would be a failure for me. If we were going to have a chance to win the game, I had to keep the ball out of the goal. Duh, but what I meant was, if you thought about it, this team, probably the best, or anyway second best in the state, was not going to give us a lot of scoring opportunities. We'd probably be very lucky to get two goals against them. So the only way we could win was if I was perfect.

And if I wasn't perfect—well, I guess that would make me the goat. This was all I could think, even though Beasley was saying something about visualizing a good performance while we sat there.

When we got off the bus, it was a little cold, and the sky was gray. "Nice day for a soccer game!" Beasley said, but her enthusiasm wasn't contagious. We walked onto the field, and we all looked around in awe. We were used to playing on like "Field F" or "Field 3-B" or something like that, but here we were on a field in the middle of a football stadium.

That was weird enough, but as we ran drills and started warming up, actual people started filling up the stands. Over on the other end of the field, we saw that the other team— Oldham High—had brought their *marching band*. Their *marching band*. For some reason, that was more intimidating than the fact that they were older and better than us.

We were used to a handful of parents in the three rows of metal bleachers, or sometimes in folding chairs on the edge of a field that had no bleachers. But now there were rows and rows of bleachers, and they were filling up with humans. And a lot of those humans seemed to be wearing the Oldham High black and orange.

The Oldham girls looked happy and relaxed as they stretched out and shot on goal and ran across the field. I guess they thought this game was a coronation.

And for us, or for me anyway, it felt like an execution.

Like all those fans in their black and orange were there to cheer on our demise.

The Oldham High marching band started playing, and their fans started cheering, and this might have completely demoralized us if it weren't for the two buses that pulled up outside the stadium. Suddenly there was a lot more blue and white in the stands. Marcia's parents unfurled a #7 ROCKS! GO CHARLESBOROUGH! banner, and I saw Mom, Dad, Conrad, and Dominic pull out a sheet they had painted to look like a brick wall with #17! GO AMANDA! graffiti written on it. It made me smile. I tried to think of myself as a brick wall, stopping every shot, but there was this little nagging demon of doubt that kept telling me I was going to let them down.

And then the cheerleaders got there. Now, I have to admit, I am as snobby as any other girl jock about cheerleading and whether it's a real sport, and you can add that to Dad's outrage about how sexist the whole thing is (they actually *bake cookies* for the football team! Like it's 1956 or something!), but I really liked hearing them yelling encouragement. Of course it wasn't enough to drown out the Oldham High marching band, but at least we had some noise on our side.

Beasley called us over and didn't have to quiet us down, because we were silent as we contemplated facing our doom. "I just have one simple message for you," Beasley said. "This is a soccer game. There are cheerleaders here, and more fans than you're used to, but nothing on the field is different from what you saw sixteen times this season. As much as you can, I want you to tune out what's happening outside the lines and remember that this is just a soccer game. And you know how to play a soccer game, and you know how to win a soccer game. Nothing has changed. You girls are awesome—you're the best team I've ever coached, and I know that sounds like a cheesy thing that every coach says to every team, but it's actually true. There is nothing—nothing at all—that will make me more proud of you than I am right now. So go out there and play your game."

We tried to cheer, but it sounded weak. I'm not sure if that's because we were too nervous to cheer properly or if we were just used to being the loudest thing on the field when there were only twelve spectators.

We put our hands in a circle and did the "One! Two! Three! Pumas!" chant, and that time we were a little louder, but still not up to our usual standard.

"Amanda," Beasley said, "take the coin toss."

I lost the coin toss, which couldn't have been a good omen for the rest of the game, and Oldham took the ball. I ran back into the goal, adjusted my gloves, and tried to shut my brain off. It wouldn't freaking shut up, though. I looked into the stands and saw my family, and, a few rows back, Lena and her family. Wow. I wasn't expecting that one.

It took me a minute to let it sink in. Was she here being punished? Were her parents rubbing her nose in it? Was she going to gloat when we lost? Was she going to be mean to me? And how must it feel to have your dad come only to the one game you can't play in?

I tried to shake it off, to stop thinking about Lena. This wasn't about Lena and me, it was about soccer. Except it was also about Lena and me, because we were always about soccer and soccer was about us. And now she was here to watch me play my worst game ever.

I looked at the other people in blue and white in the stands, the banners, and everything, trying to think about the hundreds of people who were here to cheer us on (including Angus, who apparently was a big soccer fan) instead of the one who was here to rejoice in our defeat. I guess it should have made me feel better, but as I saw the banners and the blue and white and the cheerleaders, the only thing in my mind was "You're going to let them all down."

Finally the ref blew her whistle, and Oldham brought the ball up. I guess our whole team was feeling like I felt—intimidated, terrified, and sort of sluggish—because Oldham sliced through our entire team with ease, and this girl came streaking up the wing, and all I could think of was Lena. I marked her and hoped she was going to try to fool me by going to her left foot like Lena usually did. I could see it in her feet—she was gearing up to shoot with her left, and I knew exactly where it was going. No problem.

Except that Marcia came out of nowhere with a brilliant slide tackle and sent the ball across the end line before I could get out of the goal to grab it. Corner kick.

I hate these set plays so much more than somebody break-ing away and shooting on me because they are unpredictable. A lot of teams mess up the kick, and since I'm so much taller than most of the other players, I can usually grab the ball in the air and punt it away, but I couldn't expect this team to mess it up, and if I don't grab the ball, I can never be completely sure of what's going to happen to it with all those people in front of my goal.

They set up, we set up, and everybody started moving around. My heart was pounding, but I took a deep breath and suddenly saw the field clearly. They had a tall girl right in the middle, and as the ball came shooting in front of the goal, I just knew she was going to leap up and head it at me. And I knew I was going to catch it.

And that's what would have happened, except that she must have been a little jittery or something, because she jumped early and completely missed the ball. I was still expecting it to come off her head and so was totally flabbergasted when another girl about half the size of the one who'd missed the header unleashed a *bicycle kick* and sent the ball screaming straight into the top right corner of the goal.

The game was less than one minute old.

Their crowd went crazy, their orange and black bobbing in the stands, and the marching band played some kind of exciting victory song, and the Oldham girls had these smug smiles on their faces.

I was aware of this, but I didn't really take it in. Because I was flooded with a really weird feeling: relief. The worst thing that could possibly happen, the thing I had been lying awake worrying about, the thing I had tried and failed to put out of my mind all morning had happened: I'd gotten scored on in the state championship.

And now I felt light enough to float out of the goal. I didn't have to worry about what might happen if they scored on me because it had already happened. And now that I didn't have to worry, I felt great. My shutout was over almost before it started, but now I had nothing to lose. I had no lead to protect, no more what-ifs clouding my mind.

I took a deep breath and felt my body connecting to my spirit for the first time since yoga class on Thursday night. I looked at my teammates and realized they weren't feeling the surge of relief I was feeling. Their shoulders were slumped, and they were jogging slowly back to their positions looking like we'd already lost 10 to 1.

Whatever was going on with the rest of the team, I was fired up. I decided I had to try and share some of it, so I came running out of the goal and yelled, "Shakina!"

The Oldham players looked at me like they thought I was one of those goalies who blames their teammates whenever they get scored on. They didn't know me at all. Shakina turned around and gave me a quizzical look.

"You tell those girls they'd better enjoy it, 'cause that's the last one they're getting off of me!" Shakina's face broke into this big grin, and she went running up to the front to deliver my message.

I looked around at everybody else. Some of them were smiling, but a lot of them didn't look convinced. "Hey!" I yelled. "Pumas! This is our last game together! Let's have some fun out here!"

I clapped and cheered as Shakina brought the ball up. It got stolen almost immediately, and bicycle kick girl came screaming up the right side of the field. She beat the defenders, but she was obviously so in love with her footwork that she wasn't looking for her teammates charging up the field, and, to give us proper credit, her teammates had some trouble finding a good angle for a pass.

Bicycle kick girl looked up and gave me a smug smile as she prepared to shoot. I saw the ball coming and thought for a fraction of a second that it would be really easy to punch the ball back and hit her right in the face. But as good as that would have felt, it would have put the ball back in play, and that would be bad for our team. So I caught it. I could hear our cheerleaders, and I heard a couple of my teammates yell and say, "Great save!"

Somebody—some ancient goddess of sports or something —had taken control of my mouth, because as scared and awkward and ugly as I'd felt at the beginning of the game, I was on fire with confidence and competitive spirit, and apparently that meant I had to talk trash.

"You call that a shot, Pelé?" I yelled at the bicycle kick girl. She wasn't smiling anymore. "You're gonna have to do better than that!" I punted the ball up the field and added, "Come back! I'll beat you all day long!"

I ran back into the goal pumping my fists, and I looked around at my teammates. They were running faster and smiling more. Maybe we were having fun after all.

I wish I could say we shocked them so much that we ran down and scored easily, but the fact was, this team was better than us. Pretty much the whole first half was played on our side of the field, but I didn't mind. I knew nothing was getting past me. Girls who'd been timid all season were charging the ball, cutting off the angle, and slide-tackling. They did their best to protect me, but the other team kept on coming.

And I kept on stopping them. Five shots on goal, five saves. After the fifth one, I could see the frustration building on the faces of the Oldham players. "Can't anybody on your team shoot?" I called out to them as I punted save number five up the line to Shakina.

The ref blew the whistle, and we ran over to the sideline. The Oldham girls were grinding their teeth and looking really angry. They had known exactly how this game was going to go: the lowly JV team was going to lie down and die while they rolled over us, laughing and joking the whole way. But we didn't get the memo.

As we ran over to Beasley, who was beaming, it started to rain. "Yeah!" I screamed out. "Let's get muddy!"

A few other girls took up the cheer, and pretty soon we were jumping up and down on the sideline screaming, "Mud! Mud! Mud!"

Beasley finally quieted us down and we could hear, over the crowd noise and the marching band, the sound of the Oldham High coach yelling his lungs out at his team.

"Well," Beasley said, "I was going to tell you girls to keep up the good work and have fun out there, but you're clearly all over that. You're playing a fantastic game. Keep it up."

The rain started falling harder. Our fans were chanting "Let's go, Pumas!" The time till we got back on the field seemed like it was crawling. When the ref finally blew her whistle, we went running out cheering.

Oldham looked tired and beaten down, which was the opposite of how I felt. And as fun as the first half had been, the second half was the most fun I'd ever had playing soccer.

Marcia slide-tackled again, and this time she kept sliding for about ten feet and got up laughing with half of her uniform completely brown with mud.

"That's what I'm talking about, girls!" I yelled. "Let's get dirty!"

And we did. I had three more saves, two of which had me diving in the mud and covering myself in it. After the third one, I got up smiling, and spat a mouthful onto the field. "I love the taste of mud!" I yelled. "It tastes like victory!"

This cracked everyone up, and I punted the ball way up the field to Denise, who ran by her tired, wet, demoralized defender and passed to Shakina on the wing, who tapped it in past the napping goalie.

Tie game! We were screaming, but then the ref was giving the ball to the goalie. Apparently Shakina had been off-sides. No goal. I couldn't see it too well from my position, but it sure didn't look like offsides to me.

I guess it didn't look offsides to Geezer standing on the sideline at midfield either, because she started screaming at the ref that she didn't have the sense God gave a blind mule, which must have been some kind of Texas saying or something, and how much was Oldham paying her to make bullshit calls like that. I guess that was what got her the red card.

Geezer exited the stadium, and I heard Conrad trying to start the chant of "Bulllllllshit!" but he only got it out three times before Mom silenced him.

We hadn't scored, but we had scared the hell out of the Oldham team. They spent the rest of the game playing timid, defensive soccer, so concerned with holding their one-goal lead that they'd given up trying to add to it. Girls were falling down in the mud, and I guess Oldham didn't want to risk losing the ball, so they held back and passed a lot, and their midfielders and defenders just killed time by booting it up the line and out of bounds instead of bringing it back to our half of the field.

I didn't get one more save because they didn't take any more shots. We actually got two more shots, but they were from really far away and like ten feet wide, so that hardly even counted.

Finally the ref blew her whistle signaling the end of the game, and a weird thing happened. We threw our hands up and yelled and ran around the field like crazy while the Oldham girls trudged toward their sideline and waited joylessly to get their trophy.

"Beasley! Beasley! Beasley!" we chanted, and Beasley ran onto the field and belly flopped into the mud, sliding about fifteen feet. We picked her up, and we were all there smiling and laughing and covered in mud with the cold rain pouring down on us, and it was probably the best moment of my whole life.

7

After a few minutes of yelling we calmed down, and Beasley said, "Listen. Both teams played their hearts out today, so I want you to give them a sincere 'congratulations.' They're state champs and they deserve it."

We nodded and marched up the field, telling Oldham that they'd had a good game. They were a little less enthusiastic than we were on delivering the post-game compliments. It looked like they hadn't quite realized they were state champs yet.

We lined up and stood in the rain while the commissioner of interscholastic something-or-other, some fat guy whose golf umbrella barely kept the rain off his gut, came out and gave Oldham a big trophy. They took it and headed off to their locker room, finally looking a little bit happy.

Once the ceremony was over, the field filled up with people from the stands, and my family came running toward me. I got big hugs from Mom, Dad, Dominic, and Conrad.

"That was just amazing," Dad said. "That was the best soccer game I've ever seen."

"You were awesome!" Dominic said. "Brick wall!"

"Yeah, I think it was the banner that did it," I said, ruffling his hair.

"Great game," Conrad said, already embarrassed that he'd hugged me.

"Thanks."

"It really was spectacular. We're so proud of you," Mom said. "Now go get a shower and some dry clothes on before we head over to Shakina's house."

"Okay," I said, and as I started toward the locker room, Angus elbowed his way through the crowd until he reached me.

"Hey, Amanda," he said.

"Hi!" I answered.

"Great game."

"Thank you," I said. I looked over and saw Dad staring at me, giving me the thumbs-up. I wanted very badly to give him the finger, but I thought Mom might see and get mad.

"So, now that soccer's over, I was thinking maybe you and me could grab a cup of coffee after school next week," he stammered. His face was purple again. It was kind of cute.

"Sounds good," I answered. "I like coffee." What a stupid thing to say. I fought off the urge to slap my own forehead.

"Cool," he mumbled, and disappeared into the crowd.

Suddenly Shakina appeared next to me. "Did that kid just ask you out?"

"No! He just asked if I wanted to . . . uh, hang out sometime. At a coffee shop."

"So he asked you to go somewhere with him. Alone."

"Yeah, I guess."

"I think that means he asked you out."

"No it doesn't! Maybe. I don't know. I mean, look at me—I'm like the mud monster from Planet Gigantor. He just wants to be friends!"

Shakina looked at me like I was the dumbest girl on earth. "Manda, I don't know a lot about boys, but I do know that there is no such thing as a boy who just wants to be friends."

"What if he's gay?"

"Okay. Maybe if he's gay. You think that kid is gay?"

"Well, he asked me to hang out, so he pretty much has to be, doesn't he? I mean, if he was straight, he probably would have asked you and the twins out." Or Lena, I thought.

Shakina slapped the back of my head. "You just played the best game of soccer anybody here has ever seen. Time to put that low self-esteem crap to bed."

I couldn't help laughing. "Yeah, okay."

"Good then."

Right then Shakina's mom yelled at her. "Shakina! You get your butt changed right now. We have to go!"

She smiled. "Mom's freaking out about having you guys over. She thinks you're gonna inspect the house with white gloves, so we've got to rush home and do some last-minute dusting under the furniture or something."

"No wonder she and my mom get along so well. I'll see

you soon," I said. "And by the way, that offsides call was bullshit."

"Yeah, it was. We'll get 'em next year," Shakina said before turning and heading toward the locker room, her mom yelling at her to hurry up the whole way.

I was about to go to the locker room myself, but then Lena was there in front of me. She was the only varsity member who had shown up, at least as far as I could see. I thought about how embarrassed and disappointed she must feel, and how hard it must have been for her to come out here today knowing she wasn't playing. But then, who ever said that doing the right thing was easy?

"Hey," she said.

"Hey."

"That was an amazing game," she said. "You were great."

"Thank you," I answered. "And thanks for coming. I appreciate it."

We stood there kind of staring at each other for a minute while the rain pelted our heads. I wondered what I should say next. Nothing I had said for the last month and a half had been the right thing, so why would now be any different? "Well . . ." I started, and trailed off.

"I'm sorry," she said, suddenly staring at the tops of her shoes. "I'm sorry . . . I'm just sorry for everything."

What could I say to that? It's okay? It wasn't okay. I'm sorry too? I didn't do anything wrong. I tried to imagine what Dad would tell me to say, and this is what came out of my mouth: "I forgive you."

I couldn't believe how good it felt to say those words. It was like anger at Lena and hurt at how she'd treated me was a song that had been playing in the background of my life, and when I forgave her, it turned off. It had been playing for so long that I'd forgotten about it, but the silence when it stopped sounded better than anything else in the world.

She threw her arms around me and started to cry. "I'm such an idiot. You know, me and Duncan broke up, and I've made a mess of everything."

I hugged her back and said, "I'm sorry." And I was. I didn't think she had it all coming to her because I couldn't say for sure that I wouldn't have done exactly the same thing in her shoes. I hoped I wasn't the kind of person who would do that to a friend, but then I'd never had the experience of suddenly becoming popular.

Lena pulled away, embarrassed. "Do you . . . do you want to hang out later? I'm grounded, but I'm sure Mom would be thrilled if you came over. She's done nothing since the suspension but rag on me about what horrible choices I've been making, like I didn't already know that."

"Well, we're going to Shakina's house," I said, and Lena's face fell. "But how about tomorrow?"

She smiled. "That sounds good. Call me."

"I will," I promised. I had put her number in my new phone just in case, but it was more out of superstition than hope. I felt like it would be bad luck for me to ditch her from my phone contacts even though I wondered at the time if I'd ever call her again.

I didn't know if Shakina and Lena would like each other.

I hoped they would, but even if they didn't, I probably had room in my life for two friends. Well, maybe three, depending on what exactly Angus was going to be to me.

You really can drive yourself crazy playing the what-if game. What if I'd taken Lena's number out of my phone? What if I had made varsity? What if Conrad and Lena had gone out during the summer? What if Duncan hadn't liked Lena? What if they hadn't broken up? I can't even really say that my life would be better if none of the stuff that happened this fall had ever happened—I probably wouldn't have become friends with Shakina, I wouldn't have had Beasley encouraging me to take yoga, so my heels wouldn't have gotten any better, and I might not have gotten to play in the best game of my whole life. Well, at least until I got to be the goalie on the World Cup champion U.S. national team.

For that matter, what if my birth mom had lived? I would probably never have met Mom. I might have met Conrad, but he'd probably just be some kid at school I saw in the hall. And Dominic would never have existed. Some days that doesn't seem like it would be so bad, but I really do love the little turd, and it's hard to imagine life without him. It seems like every single day, stuff is happening that can never un-happen, stuff that changes your life before you've even realized it.

You can think about all the other worlds where all these things didn't happen, or happened differently, or whatever, but why bother? You can imagine those worlds, but you can't live in them. You have to live in the real world, the world where stuff can't un-happen.

Right now that feels like a pretty good place to be.

Acknowledgments

The idea for this novel crystallized during a walk with Lori Lobenstine of femalesneakerfiend.com and her dog, Herschel. Lori also provided valuable early encouragement. Thanks to both of them!

Kate Kuhn Galle and Julie Foster Gneuss helped vet this book for female athlete realism since I have no experience playing on a girls' soccer team. Any errors in verisimilitude are of course my fault and not theirs.

Doug Stewart provided his usual awesome levels of support, enthusiasm, assistance, and friendship.

I really appreciate Janine O'Malley's careful attention to every word. This is a better book because she worked on it with me.

Last, but certainly not least, my family, Suzanne, Casey, Rowen, and Kylie were both inspiring and supportive as always. I am lucky to have them all.